THE AIRSHIP GOLDEN HIND

THE AIRSHIP GOLDEN HIND

Percy F. Westerman

Originally published in 1920.

Published by Wildside Press for release in countries where it is in the public domain.
Visit us online at wildsidepress.com.

CHAPTER I
A STARTLING PROPOSITION

"WHAT'S THE MOVE?" ASKED Kenneth Kenyon.

"Ask me another, old son," replied his chum, Peter Bramsdean. "Fosterdyke is a cautious old stick, but he knows what's what. There's something in the wind, you mark my words."

"Then you're going to see him?"

"Rather! And you too, old bean. Where's a pencil? We can't keep the telegraph boy waiting."

Bramsdean tore a form from a pad, scribbled on it the reply—"Fosterdyke, Air Grange, near Blandford. Yes, will expect motor tomorrow morning," and he had taken the initial step of a journey that man had never before attempted.

Kenyon and Bramsdean were both ex-flying officers of the Royal Air Force. What they did in the Great War now matters little. Sufficient is it to say that had they belonged to any belligerent nation save their own they would have been styled "aces"; but since in the Royal Air Force details of personal achievements were deprecated, and the credit given to the Force as a whole, they merely "carried on" until ordered to "get out," or, in other words, be demobilised. Then, each with a highly-prized decoration and a gratuity of precisely the same amount as that given to an officer who had never served anywhere save at the Hotel Cecil, they found themselves literally on their feet, relegated to the limbo of civilian life. It was not long before they found how quickly their gratuities diminished. Like many other ex-members of His Majesty's Forces, they began to realise that in smashing the German menace they had helped to raise a menace at home—the greed and cupidity of the Profiteer.

They were just two of thousands of skilled airmen for whom as such there was now no need. Commercial aviation had yet to be developed; trick flying and exhibition flights lead to nothing definite, and only a very small percentage of war-time airmen could be retained in the reconstituted Air Force.

Kenyon and Bramsdean were not men to "take it lying down." They had pluck and resource and a determination to "get a move on," and within a twelvemonth of their demobilisation they found themselves partners and sole proprietors of a fairly prosperous road transport concern operating over the greater part of the South of England.

But it wasn't the same thing as flying. Looking back over those strenuous years of active service, they remembered vividly the good times they had had, while the "sticky" times were mellowed until they could afford to laugh at those occasions when they "had the wind up badly."

Then, with a suddenness akin to the arrival of a "whizz-bang," came a telegram from Sir Reginald Fosterdyke, asking the chums to see him on the morrow.

Sir Reginald Fosterdyke had been Bramsdean's and Kenyon's O.C., or, to employ service phraseology, a Wing-Commander. On his demobilisation he went to live at Air Grange, a large old-world house standing on high ground, a good five miles from Blandford. Very rarely he left his country-house; his visits to town were few and far between, and his friends wondered at the reticence of the versatile and breezy Fosterdyke. He seldom wrote to anyone. When he did, his correspondence was brief and to the point. More frequently he telegraphed—and then he meant business. In pre-war days Air Grange was famous for its week-end house parties. The shooting, one of the best in the county of Dorset, was an additional source of attraction to Foster-dyke's guests. But the war, and afterwards, had changed all that. Few, very few, guests were to be found at Air Grange; the staff of servants was greatly reduced, the well-kept grounds developed a state of neglect. Sir Reginald's friends came to the conclusion that the baronet had become "mouldy." They wondered what possessed him to live an almost hermit-like existence. Fosterdyke knew their curiosity, but he merely shrugged his shoulders and "carried on." His work in the world of aviation was by no means ended. It might be said that it was yet a long way from attaining its zenith.

Early on the morning following the receipt of the baronet's telegram Sir Reginald's car pulled up in front of the premises used as the headquarters of the Southern Roads Transport Company. Kenyon and Bramsdean, having given final instructions to their work's foreman—a former flight-sergeant R.A.F.—jumped into the car, and were soon whisking northwards at a speed that was considerably in excess of that fixed by the regulations.

Although of a retiring disposition, Sir Reginald Fosterdyke had made a point of keeping in touch with his former officers. He had a sort of personal interest in every one of them, and on their part they regarded him as one of the best. Whenever, on rare occasions, Fosterdyke ran down to Bournemouth he invariably looked up Bramsdean and Kenyon to talk over old times. But being invited to Air Grange was quite a different matter. Vaguely, the chums wondered what it might mean, conjecturing ideas that somehow failed to be convincing. Yet they knew that there was "something in the wind." They knew Sir Reginald and his methods.

Through Blandford, up and past the now deserted hutments where formerly German prisoners led an almost idyllic existence in their enemy's country, the car sped on until it gained the lofty downs in the direction of Shaftesbury. Then, turning up a steep and narrow lane, the car drew up at the gate of Air Grange.

It had to. There was no gatekeeper to unlock and throw open the massive iron gates. That task the chauffeur had to perform, stopping the car again in order to make secure the outer portals of Sir Reginald's demesne.

While the car remained stationary the two occupants looked in vain for a glimpse of the house. All they could see was a winding, weed-grown road, with a thick belt of pine trees on either hand. To the left of the road and under the lee of the trees were half a dozen wooden huts, unmistakably of a type known as temporary military quarters. Smoke issuing from the chimneys suggested the idea that they were in "occupation," and a couple of dungaree-clad men carrying a length of copper pipe on their shoulders confirmed the fact. Somewhere from behind the trees came the sharp rattle of a pneumatic drilling machine.

Kenyon glanced at his companion.

"What's the Old Man up to, I wonder?" he asked. "Quite a labour colony. Look—air flasks too, by Jove!"

A pile of rusty wrought-iron cylinders stacked on the grass by the side of the path recalled visions of by-gone days.

"Something doing, that's evident," agreed Bramsdean. "What's the stunt, and why are we hiked into it?"

"Wait and see, old bird," replied Kenyon.

The chauffeur regained the car and slipped in the clutch. For full another quarter of a mile the car climbed steadily, negotiating awkward corners in the rutty, winding path, until, emerging from the wood, it pulled up outside the house of Fosterdyke.

No powdered footman awaited them. On the steps, clad in worn but serviceable tweeds, stood Sir Reginald Fosterdyke himself.

The baronet—generally referred to by his former officers as the Old Man—was of medium height, broad-shouldered, and deep-chested. He was about thirty-five years of age, with well-bronzed features, clean shaven, and possessed a thick crop of closely-cut dark brown hair tinged with iron grey.

He held out his left hand as Kenyon and Bramsdean ascended the stone steps—his right hand was enveloped in surgical bandages—and greeted his guests warmly.

"Glad to see you, boys!" he exclaimed. "It's good of you to come. Have a glass of sherry?"

He led the way to the study, rang a bell, and gave instructions to a manservant whom Kenyon recognised as the O.C.'s batman somewhere in France.

Sir Reginald sat on the edge of the table and whimsically regarded his former subordinates. At that moment, rising above the staccato rattle of the pneumatic hammer, came the unmistakable whirr of an aerial propeller. To Kenyon and Bramsdean it was much the same as a trumpet-call to an old war-horse.

"Sounds like old times, eh?" remarked Sir Reginald.

"Rather, sir," agreed Kenyon heartily, and, at a loss to express himself further, he relapsed into silence.

"Experimental work, sir?" asked Bramsdean.

Fosterdyke nodded.

"Yes," he replied in level tones. "Experimental work, that's it. That's why I sent for you. I'm contemplating a flight round the world. Keen on having a shot at it?"

CHAPTER II
FOSTERDYKE EXPLAINS

THE TWO CHUMS WERE not in the least taken aback with the announcement. They knew the way of their late O.C. On active service Fosterdyke was in the habit of issuing orders for certain operations to be performed without apparently considering the magnitude or the danger of the undertaking. The officer or man to whom the order was given almost invariably executed it promptly. In the few cases where the individual instructed to carry out a "stunt" failed to rise to the occasion, that was an end of him as far as his service under Wing Commander Sir Reginald Fosterdyke went. Fosterdyke had no use for faint-hearted subordinates.

On the other hand, Kenyon and Bramsdean were astonished at being invited to take part in what promised to be the biggest aerial undertaking ever contemplated. After nearly two years "on the ground" the prospect of "going up" seemed too good to be true.

"Business difficulties, perhaps?" hazarded Fosterdyke, noting the faint signs of hesitation on the part of the two chums. "Think it over. But I suppose you'd like to have a few particulars of the stunt before committing yourselves?"

"I think it could be arranged, sir," replied Kenyon. "As regards our little show, we could leave it to our head foreman. He's a steady-going fellow and all that sort of thing. It's merely a question of a month, I suppose?"

"Less than that. Twenty days, to give a time limit," declared the baronet. "Either twenty days or—*phut*! However, I'll outline the salient features of the scheme.

"Like a good many others, it arose out of an almost trivial incident—a bet with an American Air Staff officer whom I met in London just after the Yankee seaplane NC4 flew across the Atlantic—or rather hopped across. Without detracting from the merits of the stupendous undertaking, it must be remembered that the seaplane was escorted the whole way, and alighted several times *en route*. The Yankee—General U. B. Outed is his name—offered to bet anyone $50,000 that an American aircraft would be the first to circumnavigate the globe.

"Half a dozen of us took him on; not that we could afford to throw away an equivalent to ten thousand pounds, but because we had sufficient faith in the Old Country to feel assured that the accomplishment of a flight round the world would be the work of a British owned and flown machine.

"Shortly after the wager was accepted came the news that R34 had flown from East Fortune to New York in 108 hours, making the return journey in 76 hours. That rather staggered General Outed, I fancy, and he had a greater shock when Alcock and Brown covered nearly 2,000 miles between Newfoundland and Ireland without a single stop.

"Things from a British aviation point of view looked particularly rosy; then for some obscure reason our Air Board appeared to let the whole matter of aerial navigation slide, or, at any rate they gave no encouragement. The big dirigibles were dismantled and sold; powerful airplanes were scrapped, air-stations were closed, and in a parsimonious wave of retrenchment even our old Royal Air Force was threatened with ignominious relegation to a corps under the control of the War Office.

"About three months ago a wealthy Swiss—a M. Chauvasse—who had made a pile in the United States, offered a prize to the value in British money of £25,000 to be given to the first airman to circumnavigate the globe, either in a lighter or a heavier than air machine. The prize is open to all comers, and already a Yankee and a German have announced their intention of competing."

"A Hun!" exclaimed Kenyon. "I thought that Fritz, under the terms of the armistice, had to surrender all his aircraft."

"But he hasn't," remarked Fosterdyke, drily. "Nor is he likely to; and if the Allies haven't the means to enforce the terms, that's not my affair. If a Hun does compete, let him. That's my view. Providing he doesn't resort to any of his dirty tricks, there's no valid reason why the door should be banged in his face. Because he's down and out is no reason why we should continue to sit on him. Commercially, I regard German goods as a means to reduce the present extortionate prices of things in England. I'm no believer in dumping, I never was; but if our manufacturers cannot compete with the products of a country beaten in war and torn by internal troubles, then there's something wrong somewhere. But I am digressing.

"Briefly, the terms of the contest are as follows: any type of machine or engine can be employed, and as many descents as are necessary to replenish fuel and stores. A start can be made from any place chosen by the competitor, but the machine must finish at the same spot within twenty days. Again, any route can be chosen, so that full advantage can be taken of existing air stations, but—and this is a vital point—in order to fairly circumnavigate the globe, competitors must pass within one degree of a position immediately opposite the starting point. Do you follow me?"

"What is known in navigation as Great Circle Sailing," replied Bramsdean. "If a start is made somewhere on the 50th parallel North, the halfway time will be somewhere 50 degrees South, with a difference of 180 degrees of longitude."

"That's it," agreed Sir Reginald. "Now the difficulty arises where to find two suitable places answering to these conditions. With the exception of a small part of Cornwall the whole of Great Britain lies north of latitude 50.... Therefore, to reach the 50th parallel in the Southern Hemisphere would mean making a position far south'ard of New Zealand—where, I take it, there are no facilities for landing and taking in petrol.

"Nor is the vast extent of the United States any better off in that respect. I think I am right in saying that there is no habitable land diametrically opposite to any place in Uncle Sam's Republic."

Fosterdyke produced a small globe from a corner of the room in order to confirm his statement.

"And the old Boche is a jolly sight worse off," said Kenyon. "I don't suppose any British Dominion will tolerate him. It's certain he won't be allowed to fly over any Allied fortress, so where is he?"

"Paying the penalty for his misdeeds," replied Sir Reginald, grimly. "It's not exactly a case of *vae victis*. If he'd played his game, he would have taken his licking with a better grace because it wouldn't have hurt him so much."

"How many competitors are there for the Chauvasse Stakes, sir?" asked Bramsdean.

"A Yank, a Hun, and myself," replied Fosterdyke. "That is, up to the present. For some reason the idea hasn't caught on with our fellows. Probably there'll be a rush of entries later on—perhaps too late. I'll show you my little craft; but before doing so I'll give you a few details of the contest.

"My idea is to start from Gibraltar—for the actual race, of course. I'll have to take my airship there, but that's a mere detail. Why Gibraltar? Here's an encyclopedia, Kenyon. Look up the position of Gib."

"Lat. 36° 6' N.; long. 5° 21' W.," replied Kenyon, after consulting the work.

"And the antipodes of Gib. would be lat. 36° 6' S.; long. 174° 39' E.," continued the baronet. "The longitude, of course, being easily determined by adding 180 to that of Gibraltar. Now the next thing to be done (as a matter of fact I've determined it already) is to find a habitable spot approximating to the second set of figures. Look up Auckland, Kenyon."

"Auckland is lat. 36° 52' S.; long. 174° 46' E.," replied Kenneth. "Why, that's less than a degree either way."

"Exactly," agreed Fosterdyke. "The next point is to determine the air route between the two places, so as to make the best of the prevailing winds. When one has to maintain an average speed of fifty miles an hour for twenty days the advantage of a following wind cannot be ignored."

"Your 'bus'll do more than that, sir," remarked Peter Bramsdean.

"She'll do two hundred an hour," declared the baronet, emphatically. "I haven't had a trial spin yet, but she'll come up to my expectations. It's the stops that lower the average. Naturally I mean to take the east to west course. It means a saving of twenty-four hours. If I took the reverse direction, I'd be a day to the bad on returning to the starting point. The actual course I'll have to work out later. That's where I want expert assistance. Also, I want the aid of a couple of experienced navigators. And so that's why I sent for you."

"We're on it," declared both chums.

"I thought as much," rejoined Fosterdyke with a smile. "There's one thing I ought to make clear—the matter of terms."

Kenyon made a deprecatory gesture.

"Not so fast, Kenyon," protested his chief. "It's a rock-bottom proposition. Twenty-five per cent. of the prize if we are successful is your collective share. If we fail, then I'm broke—absolutely. I've sunk my last penny into the concern, because I'm hanged if I'm going to sit still and let a foreigner be the first to make an aerial circumnavigation of the globe. Now let me introduce you to the airship *Golden Hind*."

CHAPTER III
THE GOLDEN HIND

"Appropriate name the *Golden Hind*," remarked Bramsdean, as the three ex
-R.A.F. officers made their way towards the concealed hangar. "That's what
Drake's ship was called, and he was the first Englishman to circumnavigate
the world."

"Yes," replied Fosterdyke. "We must take it as an augury that this *Golden
Hind* will do in the air what her namesake did on the sea."

"Not in every respect, I hope," said Kenneth Kenyon, with a laugh. "Drake
did a considerable amount of filibustering on his voyage, I believe."

"Ah, yes," answered Sir Reginald. "Those were good old days. Now left," he
added. "Mind yourselves, the brambles are a bit dangerous."

Turning off the grass-grown road and down a side path, the two chums
found themselves entering a dense thicket that formed an outer fringe of the
pine wood.

"Short cut," remarked Fosterdyke, laconically. "Now, there you are."

A glade in the woods revealed the end of a lofty corrugated iron shed,
the hangar in which the *Golden Hind* was fast approaching completion. The
baronet "knew his way about." He knew how to deal with the dictatorial and
often completely muddled officials who ran the Surplus Disposals Board, and
had succeeded in obtaining, at a comparatively low cost, a practically new
airship shed, together with an enormous quantity of material.

"Now tell me what you think of her," he said, throwing open a small door
in the rear end of the building.

Kenyon and Bramsdean paused in astonishment at what they saw. The
Golden Hind was neither airship nor airplane in the strict sense of the word,
but a hybrid embodying the salient features of both. The fuselage, construct-
ed almost entirely of aluminium, was a full 120 feet in length, and enclosed
so as to form a series of cabins or compartments. Amidships these attained
a beam of 15 feet, tapering fore and aft until the end compartments terminated in a sharp wedge. Wherever there were observation windows they
were "glazed" with light but tough fire-proof celluloid, sufficiently strong to
withstand wind-pressure.

On either side of the hull, as Fosterdyke termed it, were six planes arranged in pairs, each being 30 feet in fore and aft direction, and projecting 25 feet from the side of the fuselage. Thus the total breadth of the *Golden Hind* was well under 60 feet. On angle brackets rising obliquely from the fuselage were six large aluminium propellers, chain-driven by means of six 350-h.p. motors.

"Some power there," remarked Kenyon, enthusiastically.

"Rather," agreed Sir Reginald. "Sufficient to lift her independently of the gas-bag, while in the unlikely event of the motors giving out there is enough lifting power in the envelope to keep her up for an indefinite period. Did you notice the small propellers in the wake of the large ones?"

"Yes, sir," replied Bramsdean. "Left-handed blades."

"Precisely," agreed Fosterdyke. "They work on the same shaft, only in a reverse direction. It's a little stunt of mine to utilise the eddies in the wake of the main propellers. Yes, petrol-driven. I tried to find an ideal fuel, one that is non-inflammable or practically so, except in compression; but that's done me so far. There's a huge fortune awaiting the chemist who succeeds in producing a liquid capable of conforming to these conditions. I even made a cordite-fired motor once—something on the Maxim-gun principle, fed by cordite grains from a hopper. It did splendidly as far as developing power was concerned, but the difficulty of excessive consumption and the pitting of the walls of the cylinder did me. However, my experiments haven't all been failures. Now look at the gas-bag."

"It's only partly inflated," observed Peter.

"No, fully," corrected Fosterdyke. "The envelope is a rigid one of aluminium, subdivided into forty-nine compartments, each of which contains a flexible ballonet. Each ballonet is theoretically proof against leakage—in practice there is an almost inappreciable porosity, which hardly counts for a comparatively short period, say a month. The gas isn't hydrogen, nor is it the helium we used during the war. Helium, although practically non-inflammable, is heavier than hydrogen. Fortunately, I hit upon a rather smart youngster who had been in a Government laboratory before he joined the R.A.F. With his assistance I discovered a gas that is not only lighter than hydrogen but is as non-inflammable as helium. I've named the stuff 'Brodium,' after the youngster who helped me so efficaciously. When this stunt's over, we're going to work the gas on a commercial basis, but for the present it's advisable to keep it a secret.

"You observe that the section of the envelope is far from being circular. The horizontal diameter is three-and-a-half times that of the vertical. That gives less surface for a side wind, and consequently less drift, while the 'cod's head and mackerel tail' ought to give a perfect stream-line."

"You carry a pretty stiff lot of fuel with those motors," remarked Kenyon.

"Rather," was the reply. "Enough for 5000 miles; which means, allowing for deviations from a straight uniform course, about six halts to replenish petrol tanks. We carry no water ballast of any description. When the fuel supply runs low, there is a tendency for the airship to rise, owing to the reduced weight. To counteract this, a certain quantity of brodium is exhausted from the ballonets into cast-iron cylinders, where it is stored under pressure until required again. The leakage during this operation is less than one-half per cent. Now we'll get on board."

Past groups of busy workmen the three ex-officers made their way. Both Kenyon and Bramsdean noticed that the men worked as if they had an interest in what they were doing. Several they recognised as being in the same "Flight" in which they had served on the other side of the Channel.

"Like old times," said Kenyon in a low voice.

"Rather, old son," agreed his chum.

They boarded the *Golden Hind*, where workmen were putting finishing touches to the interior decorations of the cabins. The floor was composed of rigid aluminium plates, corrugated in order to provide a firm foothold, and temporarily covered with sacking to prevent undue wear upon the relatively soft metal.

The door—one of the four—by which they entered was on the port side aft. It opened into a saloon 20 feet by 7 feet, which in turn communicated with a fore-and-aft alleyway extending almost the extreme length of the fuselage.

"We'll start right aft and work for'ard," said Fosterdyke. "If you can suggest any alterations in the internal fittings, let me know. It often happens that a new arrival spots something that the original designer has overlooked."

"Must have taken some thinking out, sir," remarked Bramsdean.

"M'yes," agreed Sir Reginald. "I'm afraid I spent some sleepless nights over the business. This is my cabin."

The chums found themselves in a compartment measuring 15 feet in a fore-and-aft direction and 10 feet across the for'ard bulkhead, the width diminishing to the rounded end of the nacelle. It was plainly furnished. A canvas cot, a folding table, and two camp chairs comprising the principal contents. The large windows with celluloid panes afforded a wide outlook, while should the atmospheric conditions be favourable, the windows opened after the manner of those in a railway carriage.

Retracing their steps, the chums inspected the motors immediately for'ard of the owner's cabin. Each was in a compartment measuring 10 feet by 6 feet, leaving an uninterrupted alleyway nearly 3 feet in length between.

"The fuel and oil tanks are underneath the alleyway," Fosterdyke pointed out. "I'm using pressure-feed in preference to gravity-feed. It keeps the centre of gravity lower. What do you think of the engines?"

"Clinking little motors," replied Kenyon, enthusiastically, as he studied the spotlessly clean mechanism with professional interest.

"There are six motor rooms, three on each side," observed the baronet. "I'm taking twelve motor-mechanics to be on the safe side. When we are running free, one man will look after two engines, but in any case half the number will be off duty at a time. Now, this is your cabin."

He opened a sliding door on the port side, corresponding with the officers' dining-room on the starboard side. It was a compartment 20 feet by 6 feet 6 inches, with a bunk at each end running athwartships, and as plainly furnished as the owner's quarters.

"Heaps of room," declared Bramsdean, "and warming apparatus, too."

"Yes," replied Fosterdyke, "we had the exhausts led under the cabins. Nothing like keeping warm at high altitudes. Warmth and good food—that's more than half the battle. See this ladder?"

He indicated a metal ladder in the alleyway, clamped vertically to the outer wall of the cabin.

"Leads through that hatchway," he continued, "right to the upper surface of the envelope. There's an observation platform—useful to take stellar observations and all that sort of thing. But you won't find a machine-gun there," he added with a laugh.

Passing between the 'midship pair of motor-rooms, Fosterdyke halted in a door-way on the port side.

"Pantry and kitchen," he remarked.

"I'm taking a couple of good cooks. All the stoves are electrically heated. There's a dynamo working off the main shaft of each of the 'midship motors. The starboard one provides 'juice' for the kitchen; that on the port generates electricity for the searchlights and internal lighting. Underneath are fresh water tanks and dry provision stores."

On the port side corresponding to the kitchen were the air-mechanics' quarters; while beyond the for'ard motor room the alleyway terminated, opening into a triangular space 30 feet long and 12 feet at its greatest breadth.

"The crew's quarters," explained Fosterdyke. "Ample accommodation for eight deck-hands and the two cooks. You'll notice that the head-room is less than elsewhere. That's because of the navigation room overhead."

The chums looked upwards at the ceiling. There was no indication of a hatchway of any description.

"You gain the navigation room from the alleyway," explained Sir Reginald, noting their puzzled glances. "Saves the inconvenience of disturbing the 'watch below' by having to pass through their quarters. Up with you, Kenyon. Thank your lucky stars you're not a bulky fellow. Mind your head against that girder."

Bramsdean followed his chum, the baronet bringing up the rear.

The combined chartroom and navigation compartment was spacious in extent, but considerably congested with an intricate array of levers, telephones, indicators, switches, and a compact wireless cabinet. In the centre was a table with clamps to hold a large-size chart. Right "in the eyes of the ship" was a gyroscopic compass, which, by reason of the needle pointing to the true, instead of the magnetic, north pole, greatly simplified steering a course, since those complicated factors, variation and deviation, were eliminated. Altimeters, heeling indicators, barometer, thermometer, and chronometer, with other scientific instruments, completed the equipment of the room, which was in telephonic communication with every part of the airship.

From the car the three men ascended to the interior of the envelope, climbing by means of aluminium rungs bolted to the flexible shaft. Once inside the rigid envelope, it was possible to walk the whole five hundred feet length of the airship along a narrow platform. From the latter crossways ran at frequent intervals so that access could be obtained to any of the ballonets.

The interior reeked of the strong but not obnoxious fumes of the brodium.

"Leak somewhere," remarked Kenyon, sniffing audibly.

"Yes," agreed Fosterdyke, "one of the supply pipes gave out this morning; otherwise you wouldn't know by the sense of smell that the envelope was fully charged."

He struck a match and held it aloft. It burned with a pale green flame.

"I wouldn't care to do this with hydrogen," he remarked. "Non-inflammability of the gas practically does away with all risk. When you recall the numerous accidents to aircraft in the earlier stages of the war, you will find that in over eighty per cent. they were caused by combustion. Of course, I'm referring to disasters other than those caused directly by enemy action. Now, carry on; up you go... no, hold on," he added, as a bell rang shrilly just above their heads.

"One of the workmen coming down," said Fosterdyke. "Opening a flap at the top of this shaft automatically rings an alarm, otherwise anyone ascending might stand the risk of being kicked on the head by the feet of someone else descending."

"By Jove! I know that chap!" exclaimed Kenyon, after the mechanic had descended the long vertical ladder.

"Yes, it's Flight-sergeant Hayward," added Bramsdean. "He got the D.C.M. for downing two Boche 'planes over Bapaume."

"That's right," agreed the baronet. "Jolly fine mechanic he is, too. Do you happen to know how he came to join the Royal Flying Corps? No; then I'll let you into a secret. It was in '16 that he enlisted. Previous to that he was a conscientious objector, and, I believe, a genuine one at that. What caused him to change his opinions was rather remarkable. Do you remember that Zepp raid over Lancashire? Hayward was driving a lorry that night somewhere up in the hills north of Manchester; a bomb fell in the road some yards behind him and blew the back of his lorry to bits. He came off with a shaking and a changed outlook on life. Next morning he joined up. Yes, Hayward's quite a good sort; he's been invaluable to me."

"Had any trouble from inquisitive outsiders, sir?" asked Kenyon.

"No, none whatever," replied Fosterdyke. "Touch wood. People in the village hereabouts have seen enough aircraft during the war to take the edge off their curiosity. As for our rival competitors, well, if they can pick up a wrinkle or two it will make the contest even more exciting."

"If we succeed there'll be a stir," said Bramsdean.

"Yes," agreed the baronet; "it's the first who scores in these undertakings. See what a fuss was made when the Atlantic was first flown by airplanes. If the feat were repeated, not a fraction of public interest would be directed to it. The novelty has gone, as it were. Even interest in the flight to Australia—in itself an epic of courage, skill, and determination—was limited. Sensations of yesterday become mediocrities of today. For instance, Blériot's flight from France to England: see what an outburst of excitement that caused. Since then thousands of machines have crossed the Channel without exciting comment. Now I think I've shown you everything that is to be seen. How about lunch?"

CHAPTER IV
THE DEPARTURE

"WILL NEXT MONDAY SUIT you fellows to take on officially?" asked Fosterdyke, as the chums prepared to depart. "I want a trial flight on that day, and if it proves satisfactory, I'll make a formal entry at once. M. Chauvasse stipulates that all entries must reach him in writing by noon on the thirtieth. That leaves us with only eight days clear."

"Monday it is, sir," replied Kenyon, promptly. "We'll have everything fixed up as far as our private business is concerned before then. In fact, we could arrange to join earlier—couldn't we, Peter?"

Peter Bramsdean signified his agreement.

"Hardly necessary," observed Fosterdyke. "But if anything unforeseen transpires before then I'll wire you."

During the next few days there was much to be done in "squaring up" the motor transport work. Notices were issued stating that the principals, Messrs. Kenyon and Bramsdean, would be away for six weeks, during which time all orders could be safely entrusted to their works manager. Even that individual had no inkling of the nature of his employers' forthcoming absence. The secret, jealously guarded, had not yet leaked out.

On the other hand, the Press published a report of M. Chauvasse's offer and stated that three entries other than British had been received. The lack of enterprise on the part of British airmen was commented upon and an appeal issued to sportsmen to make an effort to prevent yet another record passing into the hands of foreigners.

On the day following this journalistic jeremiad came the report that a British airship of unique design was approaching completion at a private aerodrome near Blandford, and that the Air Ministry had given instructions for all facilities to be afforded to its crew in their attempt to circumnavigate the globe within a space of twenty days. Details, both erroneous and exaggerated, were given of the mysterious airship, together with plans that were as unlike those of the *Golden Hind* as those of a modern dreadnought would be compared with those of Drake's famous ship.

"That will rattle the Old Man," declared Kenyon, when he read the announcement.

It did. Fosterdyke sent a wire asking his two assistants to join him at once. That was on the Friday morning. At 2.30 P.M.—or in Air Force phraseology 14.30—Kenyon and Bramsdean arrived at Air Grange, to find a vast concourse of would-be spectators congregated round the gates, backing up the efforts of a knot of persistent Pressmen who cajoled, bluffed, and argued—all in vain—with the imperturbable Hayward and four hefty satellites.

The grassy slopes outside the formidable fence resembled Epsom Downs on Derby Day. Momentarily motorcars were arriving, while at frequent intervals heavily laden char-a-bancs rumbled up and discharged their human cargo. Motor-bicycles, push-bikes, traps and carts added to the congestion. Thousands of people arrived on foot—from where goodness only knows! Hawkers and itinerant purveyors displayed their wares; photographers, both amateur and professional, elbowed their way towards the forbidden ground; while three brass bands and at least a dozen individual musicians added to the din. On the outskirts temporary platforms had been erected, while hirers of telescopes, field and opera glasses did a roaring trade, people willingly paying to gaze at the impenetrable barrier of fir-trees in the vain hope of catching a glimpse of the mysterious airship.

It took Kenyon and Bramsdean the best part of an hour to literally force their way through the throng. By dint of shouting "Gangway, please," they continued to make a certain amount of progress until their arrival, coupled with the ex-sergeant's efforts to make the crowd stand aside, attracted the attention of the representatives of the Press.

For five minutes the latter bombarded the chums with questions, getting inconsequent replies that put the reporters on their mettle.

"If we aren't allowed in, we'll take jolly good care you won't be," shouted one of the Press representatives, evidently mistaking Peter and Kenneth for favoured spectators.

There was a rush towards the gates. The half a dozen policemen assisting Hayward and his men were almost swept off their feet. Things looked serious. If Kenyon and his companion succeeded in getting past the gate it would only be in the midst of an excited mob.

Just then Sir Reginald Fosterdyke appeared. Some of the local inhabitants recognised him, and the report of his identity quickly spread. So when he raised his hand to enjoin silence the crowd surging around the gate ceased its clamour.

"By preventing my navigating officers, you only defer your own ends," he exclaimed in ringing tones. "The airship is not yet ready for flight, nor is she open to inspection. A trial flight has been fixed for Monday next. On that day the aerodrome will be thrown open to public inspection. And," he added, with a disarming smile, "there will be no charge for admission."

Almost instantly the demeanour of the crowd changed. There were calls for cheers for Sir Reginald Fosterdyke. Someone started singing: "For he's a jolly good fellow."

The baronet turned and hurried away precipitately. Publicity he hated. Kenneth and Peter, taking advantage of this diversion, slipped inside the barrier and found Fosterdyke awaiting them beyond the bend of the carriage drive.

"Good old British public," he exclaimed. "By Jove! They put the wind up me. I thought that they would be swarming like locusts over the *Golden Hind*. We'll have to circumvent them. Only last night some of the crew found a fellow prowling round the shed. Goodness only knows what for. He pitched some sort of yarn, and since we aren't under the Defence of the Realm Act I couldn't detain him. But this crowd scares me. We'll get out tonight, even if we have to drift, and they can have the run of the place on Monday, as I promised. But I said nothing about the airship being here or otherwise. Where's your kit?"

"Somewhere between here and Blandford railway station," replied Peter. "We saw we'd have our work cut out to force our way through, so we told the taxi-driver to take it back to the station. It isn't the first time we've parted with our kit, eh, Kenneth?"

"I'll send for it when the crowd thins," decided Sir Reginald. "Now I suppose you're wondering why I telegraphed for you?"

"The swarm outside offers a solution," said Kenyon.

"To a certain extent, yes," agreed Fosterdyke. "Apart from that, there's a reliable report that Captain Theodore Nye, of the United States Army, is starting from Tampa, Florida, tomorrow in one of the large airships of the 'R' type that the Air Ministry sold to America recently. That forces our hand. We'll have to be at the starting-point—1100 miles away—by tomorrow mid-day, so as to replenish petrol and commence the competition flight before midnight."

"And how about the Boche, sir?"

"Count Karl von Sinzig? Not a word. He's apparently out of it. Not even one of the 'also rans.' Our formidable rivals are the Yankee and a Jap—a Count Hyashi—who will reach his Nadir somewhere in Uruguay. Let 'em all come—the more the merrier."

All hands, including the workmen and mechanics who were not participating in the voyage, assembled in the large dining-hall for an impromptu farewell dinner, and to them the baronet broached the subject of the hurried departure of the *Golden Hind*.

The meal over, the task of getting the huge airship out of her shed began. Even though the wind was light the work was by no means simple. Incautious handling or a sudden change in the direction of the air currents might easily result in disaster. The operation had to be carried out after sunset and with the minimum of artificial light, since, for the present, the *Golden Hind*'s departure was to be kept secret.

With her ballonets charged sufficiently to give her a slight lift, the airship rose until the base of the fuselage was a bare three feet from the ground. The crew were at their stations, Kenyon assisting Fosterdyke in the wheelhouse, while right aft Peter Bramsdean directed the movements of the "ground-men" holding the stern, securing, and trailing ropes.

Inch by inch, foot by foot, the leviathan of the air emerged from the shed until her entire length, straining gently at the rope that tethered her to mother earth, lay exposed to the starlit sky.

"All clear, sir!" reported Bramsdean through a speaking-tube.

Curt but precise orders rang out from the navigation room. The slight hiss of the brodium being released from the metal cylinders was barely audible above the sighing of the wind in the pine-tops until the gauges registering the "lift" of the airship indicated thirty-eight tons.

Armed with a megaphone, Fosterdyke leant out of the window of the navigation room.

"All ready?... Let go!"

Simultaneously the twenty men holding the airship released their hold. That was where training and discipline told, for terrible to contemplate would have been the fate of an unwary "ground-man" had he retained his grip on the rope. But without an accident to mar the momentous event, the *Golden Hind* shot almost vertically into the air, attaining in a very short space of time an altitude of six thousand feet.

Not a cheer rang out to speed the departing competitor for the stupendous contest. Unheard and unseen save by the loyal band of helpers at the aerodrome, Sir Reginald Fosterdyke's airship was on her way to the starting-point of her voyage round the globe.

CHAPTER V
FIRST AWAY

HANGING APPARENTLY MOTIONLESS IN still air, although virtually she was drifting in a southerly direction at a modest ten miles an hour, the *Golden Hind* maintained her altitude for the best part of half an hour before any attempt was made to start the motors. She was now to all intents and purposes a non-dirigible balloon, floating aimlessly in the air.

Peter Bramsdean, his work aft accomplished, made his way to the navigation room, where he found the baronet and Kenyon watching the galaxy of lights far beneath them.

"We're drifting over Poole Harbour," observed Fosterdyke. "That's prohibited for private owned aircraft; but who's to know?"

"I often wonder what would happen," said Peter, "if a non-dirigible drifted over a prohibited area. Hang it all! The balloonist couldn't control the wind, neither can the Air Ministry, so what's the poor fellow to do?"

From their lofty post of observation, the officers of the *Golden Hind* could see the coast-line standing out distinctly in the starlight. Away to the south-east the powerful St. Catherine's Light threw its beam athwart the sky in a succession of flashes every five seconds. Nearer, but less distinct, could be seen the distinctive lights of The Needles and Hurst Castle. Then a curved line of glittering pin-points—the esplanade lamps of Bournemouth. To the south-west the lesser glare of Swanage and beyond the glow of Anvil Point Lighthouse. Lesser lights, like myriads of glow-worms, denoted scattered towns, villages, and detached houses ashore, while right ahead and for the most part visible only by the aid of binoculars, could be discerned the red, green, and white navigation lights of shipping passing up and down the Channel.

The three men watched the nocturnal panorama almost without emotion. The sight would have moved a novice into raptures of delight, but to the veteran airmen there was little new, except perhaps that in the place of star-shells, searchlights, "flaming-onions," and exploding shrapnel were the lights of a nation once more at peace with her neighbours even if not so with herself.

Fosterdyke glanced at a clock set upon the bulkhead.

"Time!" he announced laconically.

Indicators clanged in various parts of the ship. Within a few seconds the six motors, started by compressed air, were roaring. Swaying slightly under the resistance of the gas-bag overhead, the airship gathered way. In place of complete calm came the rush and whine of the wind as the *Golden Hind* leapt forward.

"May as well be on the safe side," remarked Fosterdyke. "Switch on the navigation lights, Kenyon. I don't fancy another 'bus barging into us."

He gave an order through a voice tube. Promptly one of the crew appeared from below.

"Take her, Taylor," said the skipper, indicating the helm. "Following wind—no drift. Course S. ¾ W."

"S. ¾ W. it is, sir," repeated the man, peering into the bowl of the gyroscope compass.

"Now, you bright beauties, take my tip and turn in," said Fosterdyke, addressing Peter and Kenneth. "There won't be much doing tonight, I hope, so you may as well make the best of things. If you'll relieve me at four, Kenyon?... Good."

The chums left the navigation room and made their way to their cabin. Here, although adjoining one of the motor-rooms, there was comparatively little vibration, but the noise was considerable.

"We'll get used to it," observed Peter, as he proceeded to unpack his luggage, which had been brought from Blandford station and put on board only a few minutes before the *Golden Hind* parted company with terra firma. "Seems like old times. Hanged if I thought I'd ever be up again."

"Between ourselves I'd prefer a 'bus," confided Kenyon. "Doesn't seem quite the right thing being held up by a gas-bag."

"Be thankful for small mercies, you old blighter!" exclaimed his companion. "Turn in as sharp as you can, 'cause it's your watch in four hours' time."

It seemed less than ten minutes before Kenyon was awakened. His first impression was that he was being roused by his batman, and that illusion was heightened by the fact that the man held a cup of tea.

"Ten to four, sir," announced the airman. "I've made you something hot."

Kenneth thanked the man, drank the tea, and slipped out of his bunk. He was aware as he donned his clothes that the *Golden Hind* was pitching considerably. Peter, sound asleep, was breathing deeply. There was a smile on his face; evidently his dreams were pleasant ones.

On his way for'ard Kenyon stopped to exchange a few words with the air-mechanic tending the two after motors.

"Running like clocks, sir," replied the man in answer to Kenneth's enquiry. "If things go on as they are going now, I'm on a soft job."

The first streaks of dawn were showing in the north-eastern sky as the relieving pilot clambered up the ladder and gained the navigation room. Fosterdyke, busy with parallel rulers and compass was bending over a chart.

"Mornin'," he remarked genially, when he became aware of the presence of his relief. "Everything O.K. Doing eighty, and there's a stiff following wind—force five. Altitude 5500, course S. ¾ W. That's the lot, I think. We ought to be sighting the Spanish coast in another twenty minutes."

Fosterdyke waited until the helmsman had been relieved, then, giving another glance ahead, he turned to Kenyon.

"We passed something going in a westerly direction at 1.15 A.M.," he announced. "An airship flying fairly low. About 2000, I should think."

"Not a competitor, sir?"

"Hardly. No one but a born fool would think of taking a westerly course round the earth if engaged in a race against time. We were passing over Belle Isle, on the French coast, at the time, and it rather puzzled me why an airship should be proceeding west from the Biscayan coast."

"French patrol, possibly," suggested Kenyon.

"Or a Hun running a cargo of arms and ammunition to Ireland. I signalled her, but she didn't reply. Right-o! Carry on."

Fosterdyke went to his cabin to sleep like a log. He was one of those fortunate individuals who can slumber almost anywhere and at any time, but rarely if ever did he sleep for more than five hours at a stretch. Even after a strenuous day's mental and physical work he would be "as fresh as paint" after his customary "caulk."

Left in the company of the airman at the helm, Kenyon prepared to accept responsibility until eight o'clock. He took up his position at the triplex glass window, the navigation room being the only compartment where celluloid was not employed for purposes of lighting. It was a weird sight that met his gaze. Overhead and projecting from beyond the point of the nacelle was the blunt nose of the gas-bag, the port side tinted a rosy red as the growing light glinted on it, the starboard side showing dark grey against the sombre sky. A thousand feet below were rolling masses of clouds, their nether edges suffused by dawn. Between the rifts in the bank of vapour was apparently a black, unfathomable void, for as yet the first signs of another day were vouchsafed only to the airman flying far above the surface of the sea. Already the stars had paled before the growing light. Wisps of vapour—clouds on a higher plane to the denser ones below—were trailing athwart the course of the *Golden Hind,* until, overtaken by the airship's high speed, they were parted asunder, to follow in the eddying wake of the powerful propellers.

In the navigation room, being placed right for'ard, the jerky motion of the fuselage that was noticeable in Kenyon's cabin was greatly exaggerated. It was a totally different sensation from being in an airplane when the 'bus entered a "pocket." It reminded Kenyon of a lift being alternately started up and down with only a brief interval between. Rather vaguely the pilot wondered what he would be like at the end of twenty-one days of this sort of thing.

"Bucking a bit, isn't she, Thompson?" he remarked to the helmsman, who, relieved of the responsibility of maintaining a constant altitude by the fact that the airship was automatically controlled in that direction, was merely keeping the vessel on her compass course.

"Yes, sir," replied the man. "She'll be steadier when we trim the planes."

"Might have thought of that before," soliloquised Kenyon. He remarked that the six "wings" were secured in a horizontal position. For the present the *Golden Hind* was kept up solely by the lift of the brodium in the ballonets. Not until it was fully light would Fosterdyke reduce the gas in the ballonets and rely upon the planes for "lift."

A quarter of an hour later, while Kenyon was engaged in making an entry in the log, the helmsman reported land ahead.

The *Golden Hind* was approaching the Spanish coast, not in the hostile way in which her namesake did, but on a friendly voyage across a country that, if not exactly an ally, is bound by strong ties to Great Britain.

The airship was soon passing over Santander. Ahead the Cantabrian Mountains reared themselves so high in the air that the *Golden Hind* had to ascend another three thousand feet to ensure an easy crossing.

At eight o'clock Fosterdyke appeared in the navigation room. Under his orders the airship's speed had been sensibly diminished. He intended to put to a practical test the lifting powers of the six planes.

Close behind him came Bramsdean, on whom the duties of officer of the watch devolved for the next four hours.

"Well, old bird," he observed, genially addressing his chum. "How goes it?"

"Fresh as paint," replied Kenyon, "but as hungry as a hunter."

"Then hook it," continued Peter. "The cook's dished up a sumptuous breakfast."

Kenyon made a hurried but ample meal. He was anxious to see how the *Golden Hind* manoeuvred as an airplane.

Upon returning to the navigation room, he found that the six comparatively small wings were being tilted to an effective angle, while a large quantity of brodium was being exhausted from the alternate ballonets into the pressure-flasks, until there was only enough "lift" remaining in the envelope to prevent it dropping earthwards and thus disturbing the stability of the fuselage by acting as top-hamper.

Simultaneously instructions were telegraphed to the air mechanics standing by the six motors to increase the number of revolutions.

The change was instantly appreciable. No longer did the *Golden Hind* pitch. She settled down to a rapid, steady motion, her speed being not far short of 150 miles an hour.

"No ailerons," explained Fosterdyke. "Horizontal and vertical rudders only. Saves a lot of trouble and complication of gear."

"Stunts not permissible, sir?" asked Kenyon.

"No," he replied. "They are not. We're out to do something definite, not to let the Spanish have an exhibition of an airship making a spinning nose-dive or looping the loop. But we'll do a volplane, just to test the gliding powers of the 'bus."

He touched a switch by which a warning bell rang in each of the motor rooms. This was to inform the mechanics that the electric current would be simultaneously cut off from the six motors, so that there would be no need on their part to endeavour to locate faults that did not exist.

"Cut out!" ordered Fosterdyke.

Bramsdean promptly depressed a small switch by the side of the indicator-board. This automatically cut off the ignition. The propellers made a few more "revs." and then came to a standstill. In almost absolute silence, save for the whine of the wind in the struts and tension wires the *Golden Hind* began her long, oblique glide earthward.

Suddenly Kenyon gripped the baronet's arm.

"Look!" he exclaimed. "Airship!"

Fosterdyke did as requested. The *Golden Hind* was manoeuvring high above La Mancha, the undulating well-watered plain between the Montes del Toledo and the Sierra Morena. Six thousand feet beneath the airship the town of Ciudad Real glinted in the slanting rays of the morning sun.

"Our shadow—that's all," declared Fosterdyke.

"No, not that," protested Kenneth. "More to the left."

He grasped a pair of binoculars and looked at the object that had attracted his attention. It was a somewhat difficult matter, owing to the refraction of the triplex glass in front of the navigation room, where, in contrast to the rest of the windows, fire-proofed celluloid had not been employed.

Before Kenyon had got the airship in focus the baronet had also spotted it. Apparently it had just left its shed and was heading in a south-easterly direction, differing a good four points from that followed by the *Golden Hind*.

"By Jove!" exclaimed Kenyon. "It's a Fritz! I can spot the black crosses on the envelope."

"In that case," added Fosterdyke, calmly, "Count Karl von Sinzig has stolen a march on us. He's one up!"

CHAPTER VI
Z64 SCORES

COUNT KARL VON SINZIG was certainly the "first away." Typically Teutonic, he had succeeded in throwing dust in the eyes of his rivals. Acting upon the principle "Do others or they'll do you," he was leaving no stone unturned to pull off the big prize; and, figuratively speaking, a good many of the stones were too dirty for a clean sportsman to handle.

For one thing von Sinzig had obtained his airship by fraud, although none of the other competitors were aware of the fact. Formerly in the German Air Service, the count managed to smuggle one of the Zeppelins out of the shed at Tondern, taking it by night to an aerodrome in East Prussia.

According to the terms of the Peace Treaty, Germany was to surrender all her airships. How she evaded the stipulation is now well known. The Zeppelins at Tondern and other air stations in Sleswig-Holstein were destroyed by fire deliberately, to prevent them falling into the hands of the Allies. This act of bad faith was similar to the scuttling of the Hun fleet at Scapa; and the tardiness of the Allies to obtain reparation merely encouraged the Huns to other acts of passive defiance. But, although the destruction of the airships was taken as an accepted fact, it was unknown outside certain Junker circles that one of the Zeppelins had been removed before the conflagration.

Revolutions and counter-revolutions, in which the fire-eating von Sinzig had several narrow escapes from death, led the count to seek pastures new; and about this time the publication of M. Chauvasse's terms for the international contest suggested to the Junker count the possibility of making good his financial losses.

Gathering a crew of airmen who had had experience in Zeppelins during the war, von Sinzig flew the airship to Spain, crossing Austria and the north of Italy during the night, and carefully avoiding French territory on his aerial voyage.

In a secluded part of the mountainous Estremadura he had practically his own way. The Alcaldes of the nearest surrounding villages were easily bribed to leave the mysterious airship and its foreign owner severely alone. From stores of German war material "sold" to Spain von Sinzig obtained gas cylinders, petrol, spares, and even a baby *Albatross*—a small yet powerful monoplane. With folding wings, this machine could with ease be stowed away in the car of the airship. With German thoroughness the Count, looking well ahead, foresaw that the *Albatross* would probably serve a most useful purpose in helping him to win the coveted prize.

The honour of being the first man to fly round the world took quite a subsidiary place in von Sinzig's plans. Since Germany did not own a square inch of territory outside Europe, he was compelled to make use of alien lands in which to alight. That was a handicap, and the thought of it rankled. There was some consolation to be derived from the prospect of wresting the big prize from a hated Englishman, a despised Yankee, or a miserable yellow Jap. And he meant to do it—somehow.

Already Germans had resumed their "peaceful penetration" of Great Britain and the United States. Commercial travellers, representing German houses and at the same time potential spies, were able to ascertain with little difficulty particulars concerning the British and American competitors for the Round-the-World Flight. The moment von Sinzig learnt of the date of Sir Reginald Fosterdyke's departure from England, he anticipated the time by starting the day before the British airship was supposed to leave Gibraltar.

This was a comparatively easy matter. According to the terms of the contest, competitors had to obtain a clearance certificate from an official of the International Airways Board. Provided the flight were completed within twenty days of the date of the certificate the principal condition was complied with, while it was furthermore specified that the certificate could be post-dated to the extent of twelve hours to allow for the time taken up in transmission from the Board's representative to the actual competitor.

In von Sinzig's case he scored again. Employing a swift motorcar, he obtained the official *visé* at Madrid, and was back at the rendezvous within two and a half hours, the atrocious roads notwithstanding.

Everything was in readiness for the start, and at ten in the morning Z64 left her shed and, flying at a comparatively low altitude, made off in a south-easterly direction.

The German was counting on forty-eight hours' start of his English rival—possibly more. He had been informed that the *Golden Hind* proposed leaving England on the following Monday. Fosterdyke really meant to have started on that day, and only the exuberant demonstration of the crowd outside Air Grange had made him alter his plans. It was a lucky stroke, for Fosterdyke's secret intelligence department was at fault. According to information received from Germany, Count von Sinzig was a non-starter. Incidentally it was the count who had set that rumour afloat. It was but one of the many petty artifices upon which he built his hopes of carrying off the Chauvasse Prize.

Chuckling to himself, Count von Sinzig stood beside the helmsman of Z64, quite in ignorance of the fact that a few thousand feet above him was the British airship which he fondly thought was resting in her shed in far-off England.

CHAPTER VII
DELAYS

"Avast stunting!" declared Fosterdyke. "Let's get on with it. Full speed to Gib."

Everyone on board realised that every minute was precious. With her six motors running "all out" the *Golden Hind* quickly worked up to her maximum speed of 180 miles an hour. At that rate the petrol consumption was alarming, but Fosterdyke faced the fact cheerfully. While he was obtaining the necessary certificates and making an official declaration to the authorities at Gibraltar, the airship could replenish her somewhat depleted fuel tanks.

But Sir Reginald had not taken into account the vagaries of red tape and petty officialdom.

At 11 A.M. the *Golden Hind* sighted the historic Rock. Five minutes later she slowed down and turned head to wind off the west side of the fortress. With the assistance of a dockyard mooring-party, a stout galvanised steel wire was lowered from the bow compartment of the fuselage and secured to a large mooring buoy off the Detached Mole. Then with sufficient gas in her ballonets to keep her buoyant the *Golden Hind* floated head to wind at 50 feet above the Bay of Gibraltar.

Almost before the mooring operations were completed the water in the vicinity was crowded with boats of all sorts, sizes, and descriptions, while the waterfront was packed with a dense concourse of interested spectators, representatives of the umpteen nationalities to be found living on the few square miles of thickly populated rock.

"Nothing you want ashore, I suppose?" asked Fosterdyke as he prepared to descend a wire ladder, the end of which was being steadied by a couple of bluejackets in a picket-boat.

"Thanks, no," replied Kenyon.

"That's good," continued the baronet, fervently. "Hate having to execute commissions. Not that I don't like obliging people, but I'm so deucedly forgetful. Right-o; stand by. I'll be back in less than a couple of hours, I hope. Come along, Bramsdean."

Agilely Fosterdyke swarmed down the swaying ladder, followed at a safe distance by Peter, who carried a parcel of documents and a Mercator's chart on which the proposed route was marked for the benefit of the International Air Committee's representative and also the "Competent Military Authorities" of the various garrisons where the *Golden Hind* was scheduled to land.

Peter Bramsdean had plenty of experience of petty officialdom at the Air Ministry. He well remembered the time—running into hours all told—of weary waiting in draughty corridors until it pleased certain individuals holding high places to signify their condescension (conveyed by a pert damsel in brown overall and a pigtail tied with an enormous bow) to receive the insignificant lieutenant.

Here it was much the same. The officials who were considered indispensable in the matter of signing various documents were "out to lunch."

A look of horrified amazement overspread the features of the minion to whom Fosterdyke suggested that time would be saved by sending for them. The British Empire might totter; the chance of winning fame by being the first airman to fly round the globe be lost; but by no possibility must such trivial details prevent officialdom from having its lunch—a movable feast occupying normally from one o'clock till three.

"Hang it all, Bramsdean!" exclaimed Fosterdyke explosively during one of the numerous periods of forced inaction. Clearly the usually unruffled baronet was showing signs of annoyance. "Hang it all! It was ever thus. Petty hirelings whose one idea of efficiency is to raise obstacles and to quibble over unimportant details; those are the stumbling blocks. For twopence I'd cut the cackle and carry on."

"And be disqualified at the winning post," reminded the cautious Peter. "We're wasting precious time—"

"It'll be an unofficial competition, then," declared Fosterdyke. "The honour of achieving the flight will be enough. The money prize can go hang. Come along, let's make tracks."

"I vote we look up the Commissioner at his private quarters," suggested Bramsdean. "After all, the *Golden Hind* won't have refilled her petrol tanks yet."

"'Spose not," growled Fosterdyke. "Someone's illegible signature's required for the indents, I presume. Right-o, Bramsdean, let's rout out this indispensable."

Somewhat to Peter's surprise the official was discovered with little difficulty. He had just finished his lunch, and as the meal had been a satisfying one, he was in high good humour.

"So Count von Sinzig has five hours' start, eh?" remarked the worthy representative of the International Air Board. "That's nothing. You'll make that up easily. The documents? Ah—yes—quite so. Unfortunately, the seals are in my office. I'll be along there very shortly."

"Isn't your signature enough?" asked the baronet.

The great one hesitated. On the one hand, he wanted to impress his callers by admitting that his signature was "absolutely it." On the other, years of punctilious devotion to the ethics of red tape urged him to deprecate such a cutting of the Gordian knot.

"No, Sir Reginald," he replied. "Both are necessary. One is not conclusively in order without the other. I'll be at the office by three."

It was now a quarter-past two. Fosterdyke felt strongly inclined to enquire pointedly why three-quarters of an hour would be taken up by the Commissioner in getting from his quarters to his office.

By ten minutes past three the various documents were sealed and signed. As the competitors were on the point of taking their departure the Commissioner spoke again.

"I don't seem to have seen Form 4456," he observed dryly. "That had to be obtained before you left England."

"It wasn't," replied the baronet, bluntly. "An oversight, I admit, but you don't suggest that I return to England to get it?"

"It is necessary," was the rejoinder. "Without it the flight would not be in order. In fact, as an authorised representative of the International Air Board I can rule you out of the contest."

"Piffle!" declared Fosterdyke hotly. He was rapidly nearing the end of his restraint. "This, I may observe, is a contest of aircraft, not a paper competition. Form 4456 is not an absolute essential. Since you require it, I presume the case can be met if my representative in England has the form made out and sent to you by registered post. It will be in your hands before the *Golden Hind* completes the circuit."

The Commissioner consulted a ponderous tome, chock-a-block with rules and regulations for aerial navigation, written in official phraseology so confusing that it was possible to have more than one interpretation for at least seventy-five per cent. of the complicated paragraphs.

Quoting Article 1071, sub-section 3c, the official made the discovery that the rendering of Form 4456 could be dispensed with in circumstances laid down in Article 2074, section 5c, etc., etc. Thereupon he rang a bell, summoned a head clerk, who in turn deputed a junior to fetch a certain form. When this was forthcoming a blob of sealing-wax, the impress of a seal, and the great man's illegible signature, and the trick was done. As far as the International Air Board was concerned the *Golden Hind* was a recognised and duly authorised competitor for the Chauvasse Prize.

There was still the Recognised Military Authority to be dealt with. That official was urbanity personified. He did everything in his power to expedite matters, but red tape was stronger than gold lace.

The loud report of a gun warned Fosterdyke and his companion that sunset had descended upon the Rock. The gates of the fortress were closed till sunrise.

"Won't affect you," explained the courteous official. "You can get back by the boat from the Old Mole. I won't keep you very much longer. It really isn't my fault."

"Gibraltar was a bad choice of mine for a starting-point," observed Fosterdyke.

"'Fraid so," agreed the other. "Ah, here we are. Thank you, Wilson. Where's my fountain pen? Where's— Oh, dash it all, where's everything?... That's settled, then. Have a drink before you go? No? Well, cheerio, and the very best of luck."

Armed with the necessary documents, "sealed, signed, and delivered," Fosterdyke and Bramsdean found themselves in the open air. Darkness had already fallen. It was a good two miles from Little Europa Point to the Old Mole, and not a vehicle of any sort was to be seen.

Tired, hot, and hungry they reached the spot where a naval pinnace was supposed to be awaiting them. It was not there. A message erroneously delivered had sent the boat back to the dockyard. Not to be done, Fosterdyke hired a native boat, paying without demur a villainous-looking Rock Scorp the excessive sum he demanded.

For a quarter of an hour the boat rowed about while the baronet and his companion gazed aloft in the hope of spotting the *Golden Hind* against the dark sky.

"She's gone!" declared Bramsdean.

"Nonsense!" exclaimed Fosterdyke, irritably. "Why should she?"

Nevertheless, in his mind he was convinced that such was the case.

Presently the boat ran close to the buoy to which the airship had been moored. Both men recognised the buoy by the number painted on it. No wire rope ran upwards to an invisible object floating in the darkness of the night.

Unaccountably, mysteriously the *Golden Hind* had disappeared.

CHAPTER VIII
CAST ADRIFT

ENRICO JAURES, SPANIARD ON his father's side and German on his mother's, with a dash of almost every other Continental nation's blood in his veins, lived or rather existed in a mean dwelling behind the King's Bastion, on the west side of Gibraltar.

Indolent, thriftless, and easy-going on the one hand, crafty and quarrelsome on the other, he possessed all the bad points that characterise the criminal classes of the two countries where his parents first saw the light. What he did for a living and how he earned money was a mystery even to his polyglot neighbours. Yet, without being well off, he appeared to be always "flush" with money.

Contrary to the general demeanour of the Rock Scorps, Enrico Jaures expressed no astonishment when the *Golden Hind* appeared over the high ground beyond Algeciras. He was expecting the airship, although he had to confess to himself that she had certainly arrived prematurely. Evidently this was not according to plan.

He sat, smoked innumerable cigarettes, and thought as deeply as a half-breed Spaniard can. Twice he got up, yawned, stretched himself and ambled back to the house to partake of a meal consisting principally of olives, garlic, and maize. Then back he came to his post of vantage and sat gazing stolidly at the five hundred feet of inflated gasbag riding easily to her wire cable, while her crew, bringing the airship close to the surface, were busily engaged in pumping up petrol from a tank-lighter.

The shadows were lengthening considerably when a white-robed Moor approached the reclining Jaures—a dignified, olive-featured man, wearing a thick black beard and moustache.

"The Englishman has started," observed the newcomer, speaking in Spanish with a decidedly guttural accent.

"That I know," rejoined Enrico.

"But not so von Sinzig," continued the other in a low tone, giving a furtive glance over his shoulder. "Until he arrives at Massowah it is doubtful whether he will know that this English airship is on his heels. Why is she here so soon?"

"I know not," replied Jaures. "Two men landed from her. They went in the direction of Buena Vista."

The pseudo Moor shrugged his shoulders.

"Two thousand five hundred pesetas are awaiting you in the Banqua del Espiritu at Algeciras, friend Enrico," he said in a low voice. "Prevent that airship's departure even for twelve hours and the money will be paid you."

"How can I?" asked Jaures, showing more interest than he had hitherto displayed. "I cannot place a bomb on board her, like I did on board the *Henri Artois* at Barcelona."

"S'sh! Not so loud," exclaimed the other warningly. "How you earn the money is your affair."

The supposed Moor passed on, leaving Enrico Jaures gazing thoughtfully at the British airship.

He sat and pondered until the refuelling operations were completed and the *Golden Hind* allowed to rise a hundred feet above the sea. With the setting of the sun a gentle breeze sprang up from the nor'east, causing the hitherto almost motionless airship to sway as she fretted at her cable.

He waited until darkness had settled upon the scene, then once more made his way into the house. This time he did not eat but fortified himself with a long drink out of an earthenware bottle.

Drawing his knife, he carefully oiled the blade and replaced it in its sheath. Then, having selected a marline-spike from a toolbox, he slung the implement from his neck by means of a lanyard, hiding it under his coloured shirt.

These preparations completed, he walked slowly and unconcernedly to the Old Mole.

By this time the waterfront was almost deserted. A patrol marched stolidly down the street; Enrico stepped into the shelter of a narrow courtyard until the khaki-clad party had disappeared; but before he could resume he had to await the passing of a gaitered and belted naval picquet.

The coast cleared, he reached the Mole. A tramp steamer and a few feluccas were moored alongside. Farther out a tug was engaged in shepherding a couple of large lighters alongside an East-bound liner, while changing red, white, and green lights betokened the presence of swift-moving steamboats in the bay. Standing out against the faint starlight he could discern the *Golden Hind*. Even as he looked a gleam of light shot through the windows of one of the compartments, and then another, both being almost instantly screened.

"Two thousand five hundred pesetas," whispered Jaures to himself. "A good price for a little swim."

Without troubling to remove any of his clothes, although he kicked off his canvas shoes, Enrico cautiously descended a flight of steps until his feet touched the water. Listening to assure himself that no one was about, he glided in as noiselessly as an eel, and swam with slow, steady strokes under the counter of the tramp and close to her wall sides until he gained her bows.

Taking his bearings of the airship's mooring-buoy, he resumed his easy progress cautiously lest feathers of phosphorescent spray should betray his presence.

A quarter of an hour's swim brought him up to the mooring-buoy. With considerable difficulty, for the large barrel-shaped buoy was coated with barnacles and slippery with seaweed, Enrico contrived to draw himself clear of the water.

Again he waited, listening to the sounds emanating from the airship a hundred or a hundred and fifty feet overhead. The wire hawser, acting as a conductor, enabled him to hear with great distinctness, and possessing a good knowledge of English he was able to pick up scraps of conversation between the crew. That helped him but little, for they were talking of matters as remote from the topic of the great race as the Poles.

Enrico Jaures next devoted his attention to the shackle that secured the thimble spliced in the end of the cable to the big ring bolt of the buoy.

He grunted with satisfaction when he discovered that the shackle was threaded and not secured by a forelock, but at the same time he found by the sense of touch that whoever had been responsible for the job had done his work well by securing the pin by means of a piece of flexible wire.

This latter Jaures managed to cast loose, then, with the aid of his marline-spike, he began to unfasten the shackle-pin, pausing occasionally as the strain on the wire rope increased.

At last the deed was accomplished. The shackle-pin clattered upon the rounded surface of the buoy and rebounded into the water; but almost simultaneously Enrico Jaures found himself being whisked aloft. A snap-hook at the end of a wire had caught in his belt, and there he was, suspended ignominiously like a horse being slung on board a ship, already a hundred feet or more above the surface of the sea.

His first impulse was to cut loose his belt and drop, but a downward glance at the dark unfathomable void made him abruptly change his mind.

His sole thought was now that of self-preservation. Fearful lest his leather belt should break and send him hurtling through space he clung desperately to the wire.

Fax below him the lights of Gibraltar seemed to be gliding past as the freed airship drifted towards the strait separating Europe from the African shore.

It was bitterly cold aloft. The keenness of the rarefied air was intensified by the fact that his clothes were saturated with salt water. A numbing pain crept down both arms. His muscles seemed to be cracking under the strain, while his fingers closed round the wire until the nails sunk deep into his palms.

He shouted for help—his voice sounding more like the yelp of a jackal than that of a human being. But no response came from the airship a hundred feet above him.

"Dios!" he exclaimed in agony. "This is indeed the end."

CHAPTER IX
THE ESCAPADE OF ENRICO JAURES

"WHAT ARE THOSE BLIGHTERS doing?" soliloquised Kenyon for the twentieth time. "Are they buying the place, or are they poodle-faking? They ought to have been back hours ago."

It was well after sunset. The *Golden Hind* had taken in stores and provisions and had replenished her fuel and oil tanks. An anchor watch had been set, and having "gone the rounds" in order to satisfy himself that everything was in order Kenneth Kenyon had gone to his cabin to write letters that would be sent ashore when the picket-boat brought off the skipper and Bramsdean.

A shrill blast of the voice-tube whistle made Kenyon hasten across the long narrow cabin. There was something insistent about the summons. It was not the discreet apologetic trill that the look-out man gave when he wished to report some trivial incident to the officer of the watch.

"Hello!" replied Kenyon.

"We're adrift, sir," announced the man, excitedly.

Telling the lookout to call the duty-watch, Kenyon replaced the whistle in the mouth of the voice-tube, struggled into his leather, fur-lined coat, and hurried to the navigation room. As he passed the various motor-rooms he noticed that the air-mechanics of the duty-watch were already at their posts awaiting the order to get the engines running.

Throwing open one of the windows, Kenyon looked out into the night. There was no staggering, biting wind. Drifting with the breeze, the airship was apparently motionless save for a gently undulating movement, but the merest glance served to corroborate the look-out man's words. Already the *Golden Hind*, having risen to 6000 feet and still climbing, was well to the south'ard of Europa Point. He could see the lighthouse on the south-western point of the peninsula of Gibraltar steadily receding as the airship approached the African coast.

Kenyon was on the point of telegraphing for half-speed ahead when he bethought him of the cable. More than likely, he decided, the wire rope had parted half-way between the nose of the fuselage and the buoy. There was danger in the comparatively light, springy wire getting foul of the for'ard propellers. Stranded wire is apt to play hanky-panky tricks.

"Get the cable inboard," he ordered. "Don't use the winch or you won't get the wire to lie evenly on the reel. Haul it in by hand."

Two of the crew descended to the bow compartment, which, besides forming a living-room for the men, contained the cable winch.

"'Get it in by 'and,' 'e said," remarked one of the men to his companion. "Blimey! There ain't 'arf a strain on the blessed thing. Bear a 'and, chum."

Presently one of the men returned to the navigation room.

"Pardon, sir," he said, saluting, "but we can't haul the wire in. It's foul of something. Shall we bring it to the winch, sir?"

"Foul of something, eh?" echoed Kenyon. "Does that mean we've hiked up the blessed mooring-buoy? Switch on the bow searchlight, Jackson."

The order was promptly obeyed, and the rays of the 10,000 candle-power lamp were directed vertically downwards.

Leaning well out of the open window, Kenyon peered along the glistening length of tautened cable until parting from the converging rays of the searchlight it vanished into space.

"Two degrees left," ordered Kenneth. "Good—at that. By Jove! What's that? A man!"

Filled with a haunting suspicion that the suspended body might be that of his chum Peter, Kenyon felt his heart jump into his throat; but a second glance, as the motionless figure slowly revolved at the end of the cable, relieved Kenneth's mind on that, score. Still, it was a human being in dire peril.

"Heave away handsomely," continued Kenyon. "Stand by to avast heaving," he added.

The orders were communicated to the hands at the cable-winch. Steadily the winch-motor clanked away until the word was passed to "'vast heaving." The luckless individual at the end of the wire was now dangling thirty feet below the bows of the fuselage.

It would have been useless to have hauled him up to the hawse-pipe, because there would be no means of getting him on board. The only practical way to reach him was by lowering a rope from a trapdoor on the underside of the chassis midway between the two hawse-pipes in the bows.

Meanwhile Kenyon was deftly making "bowlines on the bight" at the extremities of two three-inch manilla ropes.

"Jackson," he said, addressing the leading hand of the duty-watch, "I'm going after that chap. Tell off a couple of men to attend to each of the ropes. If I make a mess of things and don't get back, keep the ship head to wind till daylight, and then make for our former mooring. There'll be plenty of help available."

Adjusting one of the loops under his arms and another round his legs above his knees, Kenneth slipped through the narrow trap-hatch, taking the second rope with him. It was a weird sensation dangling in space with about 8000 feet of empty air between him and land or sea, for by this time the *Golden Hind* was probably over the African coast. But soon the eerie feeling passed and Kenneth, courageous, cool-headed and accustomed to dizzy heights, had no thought but for the work in hand.

"At that!" he shouted, when he found himself on the same level with the man he hoped to rescue. "Take a turn."

Ten feet from him was the unconscious Enrico Jaures. The question now was, how was that intervening space to be bridged?

Kenyon began to sway his legs after the manner of a child on a swing.

"If the rope parts, then it's a case of 'going west' with a vengeance," he soliloquised grimly. "Christopher! Isn't it beastly cold?"

Momentarily the pendulum-like movement increased until Kenneth was able to grip the arm of the unconscious man. As he did so, Enrico's belt, that had hitherto prevented him from dropping into space, parted like pack-thread.

With a jerk that nearly wrenched the rescuer's arms from their sockets, the deadweight of the Scorp almost capsized Kenyon out of the bowline. As it was, he was hanging with his head lower than his feet, holding on with a grip of iron to Jaures' arms. Thus hampered, he realised that it was manifestly impossible to make use of the second.

"Haul up!" he shouted breathlessly.

"Heavens!" he added. "Can I do it? Can I hold on long enough?"

It was a question that required some answering. The strain on his muscles, coupled with the effect of the unexpected jerk, the numbing cold, and, lastly, his own position, as he hung practically head downwards, all told against him. Even in those moments of peril he found himself thinking he must present a ludicrous sight to the watchers in the airship in the dazzling glare of the searchlight.

"Stick it another half a minute, sir," shouted a voice. "I'll be with you in a brace of shakes."

Of what happened during the next thirty long drawn out seconds Kenyon had only a hazy recollection. He was conscious of someone bawling in his ear, "Let go, sir; I've got him all right."

Kenneth obeyed mechanically. In any case he was on the point of relaxing his grip through sheer inability on the part of his muscles to respond to his will. The sudden release of the man he had rescued resulted in Kenyon regaining a normal position, and dizzy and utterly exhausted he was hauled into safety.

Someone gave him brandy. The strong spirit revived him considerably.

"Where's the fellow?" he asked.

"Safe, sir," replied Jackson. "Shall I carry on?"

"Yes, please," said Kenneth, faintly, and with the clang of the telegraph indicator bells and the rhythmic purr of the motors borne to his ears he became unconscious.

Meanwhile Enrico Jaures, to all outward appearances a corpse, had been hauled on board. One of the crew, observing Kenneth's plight, had descended by means of another rope, and had deftly hitched the end round the Scorp's body, climbing back hand over hand as unconcernedly as if he had been walking upstairs in his cottage in far-off Aberdeen.

"Like handling frozen mutton," commented one of the crew as they attended to the rescued Jaures. "Fine specimen, ain't he? An' what's he doing with that there marline-spike, I should like to know. 'Tain't all jonnick, if you ask me."

CHAPTER X
UNDER EXAMINATION

"I'M ALL RIGHT, I tell you. Hang it all, can't a fellow know when he's all right?"

Thus Kenyon rather resentfully resisted all efforts on the part of the men to keep him in his bunk. He came from an indomitable stock that never readily admits defeat, and on this occasion he steadfastly refused to recognise the fact that his physical strength had been well-nigh sapped.

Donning his leather coat, he made his way to the navigation room, staggering slightly as he passed along the narrow alleyway.

"Wireless message just received, sir," reported Jackson. "'From T.B.D. *Zeebrugge* to *Golden Hind*. Am proceeding in search of you. Show position lights. Will tranship Sir Reginald Fosterdyke and Mr. Bramsdean as soon as possible. Make necessary arrangements.' We're steering N. by W. ¼ W., but we haven't sighted the destroyer yet."

"Very good," concurred Kenyon. "Carry on."

He consulted the altimeter and the speed indicator. The former showed that the airship had descended to two thousand feet, and the speed was two thousand revolutions, or approximately thirty miles an hour. The *Golden Hind* had by this time retraced a good portion of her drift, and was now three or four miles from Ceuta.

Ten minutes later a masthead flashing lamp was seen blinking at a distance of about six miles. The light came from the destroyer *Zeebrugge*, which, pelting along at twenty-five knots, was on the lookout for the errant airship.

Kenneth Kenyon was now on his mettle. For the first time he was in command of a large airship about to make a descent. As officer of the watch, he had already had opportunities of observing the handling of the huge vessel, but now he found himself confronted with the problem of bringing her close to the surface of the sea so as to enable the destroyer to manoeuvre sufficiently enough to establish direct communication.

"Hope I don't make a bog of it," he soliloquised. "I must admit I feel a bit rotten after that little jamboree just now. Still, I'll stick it."

Although he was not aware of the fact, Leading Hand Jackson was keeping a sharp eye on his superior officer, ready at the first sign to "take on" should Kenyon's physical strength fail him.

For the next ten minutes the greatest activity prevailed. Gongs were clanging, crisp orders were issued through various voice-tubes, gas was being withdrawn from various ballonets, the motors were constantly being either accelerated or retarded according to the conditions demanded. The white flashing lamp signals were being exchanged with the T.B.D., which had now circled sixteen degrees to starboard and was steaming slowly dead in the eye of the wind.

In the floor of the bow compartment of the *Golden Hind* the large trap-hatch had been opened. Close by crouched men ready to lower away a wire rope, at the end of which a small electric bulb glowed to enable the destroyer's crew to locate the line in the dark. Throughout the manoeuvre neither the *Golden Hind* nor the *Zeebrugge* made use of their searchlights, since the dazzling rays might baffle the respective helmsmen and result in a collision.

Slowly and gracefully the airship dropped until her fuselage was thirty feet from the surface of the sea. She was now dead in the wake of the destroyer, and the task that confronted Kenyon was to bring her ahead sufficiently for the bows to overlap the *Zeebrugge's* stern. An error of judgment at that low height would result in the airship's bows fouling the destroyer's mast.

Foot by foot the *Golden Hind* gained upon the destroyer until a shout from the latter's deck announced that the wire rope had been made fast.

Instantly the airship's six motors were declutched. She was now moving merely under the towing action of the *Zeebrugge*, which was forging ahead at a bare four knots.

From the trap-hatch in the airship's bows a rope-ladder was lowered, its end being held by a couple of bluejackets on the T.B.D. Without loss of time Fosterdyke swarmed up the swaying ladder, and was followed by Bramsdean.

"Cast off, and thank you!" shouted the baronet.

"All gone," came an answering voice from the *Zeebrugge*, followed by a hearty "Best of luck to you!"

Released, the *Golden Hind* leapt a full five hundred feet into the air before the propellers began to revolve.

"Cheerio, Kenyon!" exclaimed Fosterdyke, as he joined Kenneth in the navigation room. "All's well that ends well, but you gave me a pretty bad turn. What happened?"

"Hardly know, sir," replied Kenyon. "Our wire rope didn't part. Possibly the shackle on the buoy gave. But we found a man hanging on the end of the wire."

"You did, eh?" exclaimed the baronet, sharply. "What sort of man?"

"You'll see him, sir," replied Kenneth. "He's laid out below."

"H'm!" said Fosterdyke and relapsed into silence.

He was deep in thought for some moments, then turned to Kenyon again.

"We're making an official start in a few minutes' time," he announced. "We have to pass over the Rock and display three red and three white lights to the official observer on Signal Hill. When we see a similar signal made from the Rock that will be the actual starting time. Pass the word for Jackson to get the lamps in position."

At an altitude of three thousand feet, or fifteen hundred feet above the summit of the Rock of Gibraltar, the *Golden Hind* received her official send-off at 3.35 A.M., eighteen hours after the Hun-owned *Z64*.

Evidently there was not a minute to be wasted. The contest had developed not merely into a voyage round the world within the space of twenty days, but a race in which the British competitor had to make good her formidable handicap of eighteen hours or approximately three thousand five hundred miles.

With the wind abeam on the port side the *Golden Hind* opened out to one hundred and forty miles an hour. During the earlier stages of the race Foster-dyke rather wisely decided to keep below the maximum speed, rather than overtax the motors by running "all out." Within a few minutes of receiving her official permit to depart the airship lost sight of the lights upon the Rock of Gibraltar. She was now steering E. by S.—a course that would take her over the northern part of Algeria and Tunis and within a few miles of Malta.

At 4 A.M. Kenyon, who had modestly refrained from giving any details of the part he had taken in the rescue of Enrico Jaures and had concealed the fact that he had been temporarily out of action, was relieved by Peter Bramsdean.

As he turned to go to his cabin Kenneth saw that the baronet was standing in a corner of the navigation room and studying a nautical almanac.

"Sleep well, Kenyon," exclaimed Fosterdyke. "You've some arrears to make up."

"Rather, sir," agreed Kenyon. "But we've forgotten something."

"Eh, what?"

"That fellow we found hanging on to the wire rope, we didn't put him on board the destroyer."

"No," agreed Fosterdyke, grimly. "We didn't. I saw to that. Unless I'm much mistaken our unwanted supernumerary can and must give us certain infor-mation that will rather astonish us. I'll see him later on, by Jove!"

Kenyon nodded knowingly. Evidently Fosterdyke had learnt something. However, as far as he, Kenyon, was concerned, other things of a more pressing nature demanded his attention—food and sleep.

At eight o'clock Fosterdyke ordered his involuntary guest to be brought before him.

"There's something fishy about the breaking adrift business," he observed to Bramsdean as the two sat at a table in the after-cabin awaiting Enrico's appearance.

"Where's Jackson? We'll want him. No, don't disturb Kenyon; he had a pretty sticky time."

"More than you imagine, sir," added Peter, and proceeded to tell the baronet the part Kenneth had played in the aerial rescue of the imperilled Rock Scorpion.

"Kenyon didn't say a word about it," he added on the conclusion of the narrative. "He was as mute as an oyster over it all. Frampton and Collings told me. It was—"

A knock on the cabin door interrupted Bramsdean's explanation.

"Come in!" exclaimed Fosterdyke.

In answer to the invitation entered Leading Hand Jackson, followed in single file by one of the crew, Enrico Jaures, and two other members of the *Golden Hind*'s company.

The Scorp was still labouring under the effects of his narrow escape. He looked, to quote Bramsdean's words, "as if the stuffing had been knocked out of him."

Fosterdyke's handling of the situation was a bold one. Without any preliminaries, without even asking the fellow's name, he demanded sternly:

"How much did Count Karl von Sinzig promise you for last night's work?"

Jaures gave an involuntary start, but almost immediately relapsed into his imperturbably passive attitude. Then with a slight shrug of his shoulders he replied:

"Me no spik Englis."

"Try again," said Fosterdyke, contracting his bushy eyebrows and looking straight at the man. "All I can say is that if you don't speak English it's a case of won't, not can't."

"Me no spik Englis," reiterated Jaures.

Without speaking, Fosterdyke looked straight at the fellow for a full thirty seconds. During that period Enrico attempted three times to meet the searching gaze of his inquisitor.

"Now!" exclaimed the baronet at length.

Enrico Jaures maintained silence.

Fosterdyke slowly and deliberately unstrapped his wristlet watch and placed it on the table.

"I give you thirty seconds," he said in level tones. "Thirty seconds in which to make up your mind either to answer or refuse to answer my question. Might I remind you that we are now eight thousand feet above the sea, and it is a long drop. Jackson, will you please remove that hatch?"

"Of course, the Old Man was only kiddin'," remarked Jackson when he related what had transpired to his companions after the affair was over; "but, bless me, even I thought he meant to do the dirty sweep in. He looked that stern, that it put the wind up the bloke straight away."

Absolutely disciplined, the Leading Hand obeyed orders promptly. Throwing back the aluminium cover in the centre of the cabin floor, he revealed to the gaze of the thoroughly terrified Jaures a rectangular opening six feet by four. Far below, glittering in the sunshine, was the blue Mediterranean.

"Five seconds more!" announced Fosterdyke, calmly.

Of the occupants of the after cabin Enrico Jaures now seemed to be the least interested in the proceedings. His furtive glances had given place to an expression of lofty detachment, as if he were utterly bored by the whole transaction. Bramsdean found himself deciding that either the fellow was an imbecile or else he was a past master in the art of dissimulation.

"Time!" declared Fosterdyke.

Enrico Jaures positively beamed.

"Me no spik Englis," he babbled.

Sir Reginald eyed the accused sternly, but even his piercing glance seemed of no avail. The Rock Scorp continued to smile inanely.

"Take him away," ordered Fosterdyke with asperity.

He waited till the door had closed upon the involuntary guest, and then gave a deprecatory shrug.

"The fellow's scored this time, Bramsdean," he remarked, "but I'll get to windward of him yet."

CHAPTER XI
"WITH INTENT"

"Where are we now?" asked Kenyon on returning to the navigation room to relieve his chum as officer of the watch.

It was now twelve o'clock. Bramsdean had just "shot the sun" and was reading off the degrees, minutes, and seconds from the arc of the sextant.

"Almost over Algiers, old thing," he replied, pointing to the glaring, sun-baked Algerian coast. "Hark!"

He held up his hand and inclined his head sideways. Above the bass hum of the aerial propellers came the distant report of a gun.

"Reminds a fellow of old times when the Archies got busy," remarked Kenyon.

"Our friends the French are evidently treating us to a salute to help us on our weary way," rejoined Peter. "Goodness only knows how we are to return it. We can't give gun for gun."

He focussed his glasses on the white buildings three thousand feet below. The whole of the waterfront of Algiers was packed with figures with upturned faces—Frenchmen, Algerines, Arabs, and Nubians—all frantically waving to the huge airship as she sped eastwards.

In ten minutes the *Golden Hind* had left the capital of France's African possessions far astern. Unless anything untoward occurred, another four hours would bring her within sight of Malta.

"You might cast your eye over the signal logbook before you take on," remarked Bramsdean.

Kenyon did so. Evidently the wireless operator had been kept busily employed, for there were dozens of messages wishing the *Golden Hind* bon voyage. But amongst them were two of a different nature. One announced that an American airship "Eagle," under the command of Commodore Theodore Nye, had left Tampa Town bound for Colon, followed by a supplementary message that the "Eagle" had left the Panama Canal zone and was last sighted flying in a westerly direction. Making allowance for the difference in New York and Greenwich times, both the *Golden Hind* and her Yankee rival had started practically simultaneously from their respective points of departure for the actual race.

The second wireless message, transmitted via Vancouver, Newfoundland, and Poldu, was to the effect that the *Banzai*, the Japanese quadruplane piloted by Count Hyashi, had started from Nagasaki at a speed estimated at two hundred and twenty miles an hour.

"Artful blighter, that Jap," declared Bramsdean. "He's kept his design carefully up his sleeve till the last moment. We thought he was attempting the flight in an airship, but he's pinned his faith to a gigantic quadruplane."

"Two hundred and twenty miles an hour, too," added Kenyon. "That means he'll do the whole trip in less than 120 hours of actual flying, unless something goes wrong with his 'bus. My word, some speed!"

"What I'd like to know is his petrol consumption, and how much juice does his 'bus carry," remarked Bramsdean, thoughtfully. "By Jove! We're up against something, old son."

"By the by, I see there's no news of Fritz," said Kenneth.

"Not a word," replied Peter. "Von Sinzig evidently thinks that it's too early to start bragging. We'll hear either from or of him before night. Fosterdyke is trying to call him up by wireless and tell him that he has a friend of his on board."

"Oh, that greasy merchant!" rejoined Kenneth. "How did he get on?"

"Played 'possum," answered Bramsdean. "Fosterdyke tried to put the wind up him, but it was a frost. I'd like to know what he did to the shackle on the mooring-buoy."

"You think he cast us adrift?"

"Without a doubt, old bird."

Kenyon shook his head doubtfully.

"He might have been simply fishing when the pin drew and he got whisked aloft," he suggested. "Did he give his name or any particulars?"

"Not he," replied Peter. "In fact he wasn't asked. Fosterdyke went for him bald-headed and tried to make him admit that he was in von Sinzig's pay. But nothin' doin', even when we made out that we were going to drop him overboard. Well, cheerio, old thing."

Left in charge of the airship, Kenyon pondered over the problem of whether the man he had rescued had really been a secret agent of von Sinzig or otherwise. If he were, then it would be almost a foregone conclusion that he spoke German.

Kenneth had plenty of time for reflection during his "trick." The *Golden Hind* was making good progress. There was little or no wind, and her drift was in consequence almost imperceptible; while the temperature was so constant that there was no necessity to alter the volume of brodium in the ballonets for hours at a stretch. The motors, too, ran like clockwork, and beyond attending to the semi-automatic lubricators occasionally, the air-mechanics on duty had little to do. Fosterdyke, having paid a brief visit to the navigating room, retired to his cabin to make up arrears of sleep.

"Might work," soliloquised Kenneth, reflectively. "I'll tackle Fosterdyke about it next time I come across him."

At four in the afternoon Malta was passed at a distance of ten miles to the south'ard. The *Golden Hind* was doing well, maintaining more than her normal cruising speed. If she were able to keep on at that rate she would accomplish the voyage of circumnavigation well under the twenty days; but that was now but a secondary consideration. At all costs von Sinzig's Z64 must be overhauled.

The *Golden Hind*'s first stop was at Alexandria, sixteen hours after leaving Gibraltar. She made a faultless landing on sandy spit that separates Lake Mareotis from the Mediterranean. The time of her arrival had been notified by wireless, and all preparations had been made for her reception. Keenly interested Tommies manned the trail ropes and secured her firmly to anchors buried in the sand; lorries laden with petrol and oil were rushed to the spot, and the work of refuelling began without delay. While Fosterdyke and Kenyon were signing the "control certificate" and holding an informal reception of almost the whole of the British Colony at Alexandria, Bramsdean remained in charge of the airship.

In order to keep back the dense crowd, composed of fellaheen, Copts, Arabs, Syrians, and representatives of every nation bordering on the Mediterranean, strong picquets of British troops were posted round the tethered airship, no unauthorised person being permitted to approach within a hundred yards of the *Golden Hind*; while to enable the work of refuelling to proceed as rapidly as possible, the improvised aerodrome was brilliantly illuminated by portable searchlights mounted on motor lorries.

It seemed as if it would be impossible for any suspicious characters to approach the airship without being detected. Having once been "bitten," Fosterdyke was not taking chances in that direction.

No attempt had been made to get rid of Enrico Jaures. Closely watched by a couple of the crew, he was even permitted to view the proceedings from an open scuttle in one of the compartments on the starboard side.

When everything was in readiness to resume the voyage, Fosterdyke and Kenyon shook hands with their entertainers and crossed the guarded square. As they approached the entry port on the starboard side a dark figure suddenly appeared from behind an unattended lorry, and at a distance of ten paces fired half a dozen shots in rapid succession straight at the baronet.

Almost at the first report Fosterdyke threw himself at full length upon the sand. Kenyon, without hesitation, rushed upon the would-be assassin, while two of the crew, leaping from the fuselage, promptly seized the miscreant and deprived him of his automatic pistol.

"Hurt, sir?" asked Kenyon, anxiously.

"Not a bit of it," replied Sir Reginald coolly. "That fellow couldn't hit a haystack at five yards. Bring him along, men."

An agitated member of the Egyptian Civil Service, accompanied by a couple of staff officers, hurried up, and after making inquiries and learning that Fosterdyke was unhurt, suggested, not without good reason, that the would-be assassin should be handed over to the civil powers for trial.

The baronet airily swept aside the suggestion.

"Sorry, Vansittart," he said; "but I'm not going to waste precious time appearing as a prosecutor in this business. No, I'm not exactly professing to take the law into my own hands, but I propose taking the gentleman with me. If he tried to shoot me, surely I can jolly well kidnap him. 'Tany rate, possession's nine points of the law. When I've done with him you can deal with him."

"But, dash it all, man!" exclaimed one of the staff officers; "you aren't going to—to—"

"Hang him? Not much," declared the baronet. "Return good for evil sort of thing, you know. Don't get flustered, Vansittart. He's mine, and we're just off."

Happening to glance up as he entered the fuselage, Fosterdyke caught sight of Enrico Jaures, who had seen the whole incident through one of the windows.

"Birds of a feather," he soliloquised. "However, I don't suppose we'll pick up pals of this sort at every place we touch. All ready, Kenyon?" he asked, raising his voice. "Right-o; let go."

CHAPTER XII
CONFIDENCES

IN ONE OF THE store-rooms, the contents of which had been removed in order to adapt the place to present requirements, sat Enrico Jaures and the would-be assassin. They were under lock and key and had been unceremoniously bundled into durance vile without the formality of an introduction.

Enrico was feeling fairly content, in spite of being a prisoner. After all, he reflected, nothing had been proved against him. He had scored in his encounter with the captain and owner of the British airship, and, all things considered, he was being well treated.

He made no remark when his new companion was gently but firmly propelled through the doorway. The newcomer was equally reticent; so the ill-assorted pair—one rigged out in the nondescript garments of a low-class inhabitant of Gibraltar and the other in European clothes and a tarboosh—sat in opposite corners of the limited space.

For the best part of an hour neither spoke. Occasionally they regarded each other furtively. Then the gentleman who had demonstrated so effectively how not to shoot straight began to slumber. Sitting on his haunches with his arms clasped round his bent knees, he nodded his crimson tarboosh until his head found a rather uncomfortable resting-place on his clasped hands.

Then in his somnolent condition he began muttering his wandering sentences, punctuated with many "Achs!"

Enrico listened intently. Hitherto he had been in ignorance of the motive that had prompted the would-be murderer. Now he had enough evidence to form the conclusion that they both had a motive in common—to wreck the attempt of the British competitor to win the Chauvasse Prize.

Nevertheless Jaures was of a cautious disposition, and when his companion awoke he still maintained his attitude of aloofness.

Breakfast time came. One of the *Golden Hind*'s crew appeared with quite a substantial meal, and both men were hungry. The pure, cold air, a striking contrast to the hot, enervating atmosphere of Alexandria, had given them an enormous appetite, and the fact that they had to share their meals and were not provided with knives and forks did not trouble them.

"Pass the salt," said Enrico's companion, speaking in German.

Jaures complied without hesitation. The request was so natural that it took him completely off his guard.

"So you do speak German," remarked the wearer of the tarboosh.

Enrico shook his head.

"Come, come," continued the other. "Do not say that you cannot. I asked you for the salt. I was not looking at it, so that you have no excuse."

Jaures swallowed a big chunk of bread and stole cautiously to the door. For a few seconds he listened lest there should be anyone eavesdropping without.

"Yes," he admitted. "My mother was German. But don't speak so loudly."

"From what town came she?" asked his companion.

"From Lubeck," he replied.

"And I come from Immeristadt. I am a Swabian and my name is Otto Freising," announced the German. "What are you doing here?"

"I am not here of my own free will," said Jaures, guardedly. He was rather inclined to shut up like an oyster, but his semi-compatriot was persistent.

"I suppose these Englishmen will hang me," remarked Otto. "My one regret is that I did not succeed in my attempt."

"What attempt?" asked Enrico, innocently. As a matter of fact he knew, having watched the shooting affray.

Otto told him.

"The trouble is," he added, "I've been paid for this business. Ten thousand Egyptian piastres. I have a banker's order for that amount in my pocket. Will they search me?"

"Without a doubt," replied Enrico, whose knowledge of British criminal courts was of a first-hand order. "But in a way you are lucky. You were paid—I was not. I succeeded—you failed."

The German raised his eyebrows, but forbore to elicit further information concerning Jaures' motives.

"My difficulty," resumed Otto, "is what I am to do with this banker's order. I undertook the business because I was hard up, and should I be hanged or even imprisoned my family will not benefit because the money will be confiscated."

He paused. Enrico eyed him thoughtfully. He would willingly rob anybody. Now was a chance of enriching himself at the expense of his semi-compatriot.

"These English cannot keep me in captivity much longer," he observed. "They can prove nothing against me. When I regain my liberty I propose paying a visit to my mother's relations in Lubeck. Perhaps I might be able to render you a service by handing that draft to your relatives."

Otto showed no great eagerness to close with the offer. His hesitation increased his companion's cupidity.

"Rest assured that the money will eventually reach a safe destination," he urged enigmatically. "Better even to run the risk of its being lost than to let it fall into the hands of these Englishmen."

"That is so," agreed Otto. "At any rate I can entrust it in your keeping for the next few days until I know what they propose doing with me. You will, of course, be paid well for your trouble."

Enrico waved his hands deprecatingly, swearing by his patron Saint Enrico of Guadalajara that it would be a pleasure and a duty to assist a German in distress.

"Very well, then," agreed Otto, producing a paper from the double crown of his tarboosh.

The Rock Scorp, craftily concealing his delight at the success of his plan, took the document and glanced at the amount written thereon. As he did so he uttered an exclamation.

"Dios!" he said.

"What is it?" asked Otto.

"The signature—Hans von Effrich. I know the man. He was at Barcelona when the U-boats were busy. I helped him to—"

He broke off abruptly, realising, perhaps, that there were limits to an exchange of confidences.

"Von Effrich—I have never met him," declared Otto. "All I know is that he is now an agent for Count Karl von Sinzig."

"Where is he now?" asked Jaures.

"Who?—von Sinzig or von Effrich?"

"Von Effrich."

"He is usually to be found in Corinth," replied Otto. "Why do you ask?"

"Because he might also pay me what von Sinzig owes me," replied Enrico. "We apparently are engaged on similar tasks."

"To cripple or delay this airship," added Otto. "Up to the present we have not made much of a success of it. My prospects are not at all bright, but my one hope is that when we arrive at Singapore von Blicker will be there. A clever fellow, von Blicker. I met him at von Effrich's house just before I left Corinth for Alexandria—a month ago."

"What is he going to do?" asked Enrico.

"I believe he'll— Shh! someone coming."

CHAPTER XIII
THE TAIL OF A CYCLONE

"HANGED IF I LIKE the look of things one little bit," declared Fosterdyke, frankly. "Glass dropping as quickly as if the bottom of it had fallen out, and on top of it all we get this."

"This" was a wireless from Point de Galle announcing that a terrific cyclone was raging west of the Maldive Islands, its path being a "right-hand circle." That meant that unless the *Golden Hind* made a radical alteration of course she would encounter the full force of the wind.

It was the fourth day of the race. The *Golden Hind* had passed over Socotra at daybreak and was on her way across the Arabian Sea, her next scheduled landing-place being Colombo.

"If we carry on we'll hit the tail of the cyclone," said Kenyon, consulting a chart of the Indian Ocean.

"Yes, but what is worse we'd pass through the dangerous storm-centre, and then more than likely get a nose-ender on the other side, if we were lucky enough to weather the centre," replied Fosterdyke. "It's too jolly risky, Kenyon. At fifteen thousand feet it may be as bad or worse than at five hundred feet up. Call up Murgatroyd, and ask what petrol there is in the tanks."

Kenneth went to the voice tube and made the necessary enquiry of the engineer.

"By Jove, we'll risk it!" declared Fosterdyke, when he received the desired information. "We'll go south a bit, and then make straight for Fremantle."

Kenyon was taken aback with the audacity of the proposal. The distance between Socotra and Western Australia was a good 5000 miles, or thirty-six hours of uninterrupted flight. At 140 miles an hour there was sufficient fuel on board for forty hours, which meant a reserve of four hours only in case of anything occurring to protract the run.

"Oh, we'll do it," said Fosterdyke, confidently, as he noticed his companion's look of blank amazement. "Better run the risk of cutting things fine than to barge into a cyclone. Sou'-east by south is the course."

"Remarkable thing we haven't heard anything of friend Sinzig 'clocking in,'" observed Kenyon. "Wonder where he's making for?"

"We'll hear in due course," replied the baronet. He crossed the cabin to consult a Mercator's chart of the world, on which were pinned British, American, and Japanese flags recording the latest-known positions of the rival airmen. There was a German flag ready to be stuck in, but nearly five days had elapsed since von Sinzig left Spain, and the crew of the *Golden Hind* were still in ignorance of his whereabouts.

But they had the satisfaction of knowing that they more than held their own with the others. The American had passed the Azores, while Count Hyashi's *Banzai*, which had made a stupendous non-stop flight to Honolulu, had developed engine defects that promised to detain him indefinitely.

"Two thousand miles in nine hours," remarked Fosterdyke, referring to the Japanese airplane's performance. "Some shifting that, but Count Hyashi has evidently gone the pace a bit too thick. He's our most dangerous rival, Kenyon."

"Unless von Sinzig has something up his sleeve, sir," added Kenneth.

"Trust him for that," said the baronet, grimly. "However, time will prove. Well, carry on, Kenyon. Call me if there's any great change in the weather."

Within the next two hours there were indications that even the new course taken by the *Golden Hind* would not allow her to escape the cyclone. Right ahead the hitherto cloudless sky was heavy with dark, ragged thunderclouds that, extending north and south as far as the eye could see, threatened to close upon the airship like the horns of a Zulu impi.

Roused from his sleep, Fosterdyke lost no time in making his way to the navigation room. Although he was not to be on duty for another hour and a half, Peter Bramsdean had also hurried to the chartroom.

"We're in for it, sir," declared Kenneth.

"We are," agreed Fosterdyke, gravely. "Evidently there is a second disturbance, but judging from appearances it's none the less formidable. No use turning tail. We'll go up another five thousand feet and see what it looks like."

The *Golden Hind* rose rapidly, under the joint action of her six planes and the addition of brodium to the ballonets; but even then it was touch-and-go whether the gathering storm would encircle her. As it was she flew within the influence of the fringe of the cyclone. Shrieking winds assailed her, seeming to come from two opposing quarters. Her huge bulk lurched and staggered as she climbed. Her fuselage see-sawed as the blast struck the enormous envelope above, while the jar upon the tension wires was plainly felt by the crew.

For a full ten minutes it was as black as night, save when the dark masses of cloud were riven by vivid flashes of lightning. Blinded by the almost incessant glare, Fosterdyke and his companions could do little or nothing but hang on, trusting that the *Golden Hind* would steer herself through the opaque masses of vapour. It was impossible to consult the instruments. Whether the airship was rising or falling, whether she was steering north, south, east, or west remained questions that were incapable of being solved, since the blinding flashes of lightning and the deafening peals of thunder literally deprived the occupants of the navigation room of every sense save that of touch. All they could do was to hold on tightly, clench their teeth, and wait.

It required some holding on. At one moment the longitudinal axis of the airship was inclined at an angle of forty-five degrees; at another she was heeling to almost the same angle, the while twisting and writhing like a trapped animal. Now and again she seemed to be enveloped in electric fluid. Dazzling flashes of blue flame played on and along the aluminium envelope, vicious tongues of forked lightning seemed to stab the gas-bag through and through; and doubtless had the ballonets contained hydrogen instead of non-inflammable brodium the *Golden Hind* would have crashed seawards in trailing masses of flame.

How long this inferno lasted no one on board had the remotest idea. The flight of time remained a matter of individual calculation. To Kenyon it seemed hours; Bramsdean afterwards confessed that he thought the passage through the storm cloud lasted thirty minutes. In reality only six minutes had elapsed from the time the *Golden Hind* was enveloped in the thunder cloud till the moment when she emerged.

It was much like being in a train coming out of a long tunnel. With their eyes still dazed by the vivid flashes the men in the navigation room became aware that the vapour was growing lighter. They could distinguish the smoke-like rolls of mist as the sunshine penetrated the upper edges of the clouds. Then, no longer beaten by the torrential downpour of hail, the *Golden Hind* shot into a blaze of brilliant sunshine.

It seemed too good to be true. For some moments Fosterdyke and his companions simply stared blankly ahead until their eyes grew accustomed to the different conditions.

Then Kenyon, who was still officer of the watch, glanced over the shoulder of the helmsman and noted the compass. The lubber's line was a point west of north. The *Golden Hind* had been practically retracing her course and might be anything from fifty to a hundred miles farther away from her goal than she had been when the storm enveloped her.

Obedient to the action of the vertical rudders the airship swung back on her former course. The altimeter indicated a height of twelve thousand feet, and the *Golden Hind* was still rising. Three thousand feet below was an expanse of wind-torn clouds, no longer showing dark, but of a dazzling whiteness. The crew of the *Golden Hind* were literally looking on the bright side of things.

"We're well above the path of the storm," remarked Fosterdyke, gratefully. "We've a lot to be thankful for, but the fact remains we daren't descend while that stuff's knocking about. Once in a lifetime is quite enough."

Before any of his companions could offer any remark, Murgatroyd, the chief air-mechanic on duty, appeared through the hatchway.

"Sorry to have to report, sir," he announced, "that the two after motors are both out of action. Blade smashed on the starboard prop, sir, and the chain-drive on the port prop has snapped. The broken chain is in your cabin, sir."

"Who put it there?" asked Fosterdyke.

"It put itself there, sir," was the imperturbable reply. "Sort of flew off the sprocket when the link parted and went bang through the side plate of the fuselage, sir. I'll allow it's made a wee bit of a mess inside, sir."

"Take over, Bramsdean, please," said Fosterdyke. "Directly you get a chance obtain our position. Come on, Kenyon, let's see the extent of the damage. The cabin doesn't matter. It isn't the first time I've slept in a punctured dog-box. But the mechanical breakdown—that's the thing that counts."

Followed by Murgatroyd, the baronet and Kenyon went aft. From No. 5 motor-room they could see the motionless propeller, one of the four blades of which had been shattered as far as the boss, while all the others bore signs of more or less damage from the flying fragments.

"Matter of twenty minutes, sir," replied Murgatroyd in answer to his chief's enquiry as to how long the repairs would take. "We'll have to stop, and I'll bolt on the new blades. At the same time I'll put a couple of hands on to fitting a new chain to the starboard drive. I don't fancy the 'A' bracket's strained, but I'll soon find out directly we stop."

It was rough luck to have to stop all the motors and drift at the mercy of the air currents for twenty precious minutes; but the only option would be to carry on under the action of four propellers only at a greatly reduced speed.

"Right-o, Murgatroyd," agreed the baronet. "Slap it about."

"Trust me for that, sir," replied the engineer. "I've warned the break-down gang. I'll give you the all-clear signal in twenty minutes—less, sir, or my name isn't Robert Murgatroyd."

Three minutes later the remaining four motors were switched off, and the *Golden Hind*, rapidly losing way, fell off broadside on to the wind at a height of twelve thousand five hundred feet above sea-level.

Instantly the mechanics swarmed out along the slender "A" brackets, Murgatroyd and an assistant setting to work to unbolt the damaged blades, while other airmen passed a new chain round the sprocket wheels of the starboard motor and propeller respectively.

Although there was no apparent wind, and the airship was drifting at practically the same rate as the air current, it was bitterly cold. The brackets were slippery with ice, and the difficulty of maintaining a foothold was still further increased by the erratic vertical motion of the airship.

The mechanics, wearing lifelines, went about their work fearlessly. They were used to clambering about on coastal airships, sometimes under fire; and although the present task was a simple one from a mechanical point, it was most difficult owing to the adverse atmospheric conditions.

Yet in the space of seventeen and a half minutes Murgatroyd and his band of workers were back in the fuselage, their task accomplished, and in twenty minutes the six motors were running once more.

Murgatroyd flushed with pleasure when his chief thanked and complimented him.

"Maybe, sir, you'd be liking to have your cabin repaired?" he asked. "Just a sheet of metal strapped against the plates will hold till we land again. Then I'll see that it's well bolted on, sir; but I'll guarantee you'll not be feeling the draught tonight."

CHAPTER XIV
THE BOAT'S CREW

THE STATE OF HIS cabin hardly troubled Fosterdyke. He never even went to investigate the extent of the damage, for the moment the airship's motors were re-started he hastened back to the navigation room.

"Got a fix yet, Bramsdean?" were his first words.

Peter handed him a slip of paper.

"Well out of our course, sir," he remarked.

The position was given as lat. 3° 15' 20" S., long. 58° 20' 5" E.

"We are," agreed Fosterdyke gravely. "Well to the west'ard. We ought to be within sight of the Seychelles."

"Any chance of getting petrol there, I wonder?" asked Bramsdean. "Judging by the name it seems a likely place to get 'Shell brand.'"

"Don't prattle, Peter," exclaimed Kenneth, facetiously.

Fosterdyke laughed at the joke.

"Rotten puns, both of them," he said. "All the same I wish we had another two hundred gallons of 'Pratt's' or 'Shell' or any other old brand of petrol. But it's no use going still farther out of our course on the off chance of getting juice, so we'll just carry on."

With the passing of the cyclone the wind fell light. What little there was was dead aft. The sea, viewed from an altitude of three thousand feet, appeared as smooth as glass, although in reality there was a long rolling ground swell.

In order to economise the petrol consumption, the speed of the *Golden Hind* was reduced to ninety miles an hour. Should the favouring wind hold, the airship stood a good chance of making the Australian coast. If it changed and blew from the south-east, then Fosterdyke's chances of winning the race would be off.

Just before eleven o'clock in the morning of the day following the storm, Frampton, one of the crew on duty in the navigation room, reported a boat about three miles away on the port bow.

By the aid of glasses, it was seen that the boat was a ship's cutter moving slowly under sail in an easterly direction. Her crew were hidden from view by a spare sail rigged as an awning over the stern sheets.

"Something wrong there," remarked Bramsdean. "A small boat hundreds of miles from the nearest land requires some explanation. Inform Sir Reginald, Frampton; tell him I propose coming down within hailing distance."

Before Fosterdyke could reach the navigation room the noise of the *Golden Hind*'s aerial propellers had attracted the attention of the occupants of the cutter, and six or seven men, whipping off the awning, began waving strips of canvas and various garments.

Slowing down and descending to fifty feet, the airship approached the boat. The latter was hardly seaworthy. Her topstrake had been stove in on the starboard side and had been roughly repaired by means of a piece of painted canvas. Her sails were patched in several places, while in default of a rudder she was being steered by means of an oar.

"Poor chaps! Look at them!" said Kenneth. "They're almost done in."

The boat's crew were indeed in desperate straits. They were ragged, gaunt, and famished. Their faces and hands were burnt to a brick-red colour with exposure to the wind and tropical sun. Three of them, seeing that help was at hand, had collapsed and were lying inertly on the bottom-boards.

Viewed from a height of fifty feet the length of the ocean rollers became apparent. The sea was not dangerous, since there were no formidable crests to the long undulations, but there was considerable risk of the lightly built fuselage sustaining damage should the boat surge alongside. On the other hand, it was almost a matter of impossibility to get the men on board otherwise than by the airship descending and resting on the surface. Obviously they were far too weak to attempt to climb the rope-ladder, while the use of bowlines was open to great objection both as regards the length of time and the risk of injury to the rescued men.

Being a ship's boat the cutter was provided with slinging gear. The question was whether in her damaged state the boat would break her back in being hoisted; but Fosterdyke decided to take the risk.

Accordingly wire hawsers were lowered from the two bow-hawser pipes, and by dint of careful manoeuvring the shackles were engaged. Then, under the lifting power of additional brodium introduced into the for'ard ballonets, the *Golden Hind* rose vertically until the boat was clear of the water. The motor winches were then started and the cutter hauled up until her gunwales were almost touching the underside of the airship's nacelle.

One by one the exhausted men were taken on board the airship by means of the hatchway through which Kenyon had gone to the rescue of Enrico Jaures.

This done, two of the *Golden Hind*'s men dropped into the boat and passed slings round her. When these took the weight of the cutter the wire hawsers were unshackled and the two men clambered back to the airship, which had now risen to nearly a thousand feet. One end of each sling was then slipped, and the boat, falling like a stone, splintered to matchwood as she struck the surface of the sea.

The seven rescued men were given food and drink in strictly moderate quantities. Vainly they begged for more, but Fosterdyke knew the danger of starving men being allowed to eat and drink their fill. Nor did he attempt to question them at that juncture, beyond ascertaining that there were no more boats belonging to their ship. They were put into bunks and made to sleep.

It was not until ten o'clock on the following morning that four of the rescued men put in an appearance in Fosterdyke's cabin. The remaining three were too ill to leave their bunks.

They were, they said, the sole survivors of the American barque *Hilda P. Murchison*, thirty days out from Albany, Western Australia, and bound for Karachi. Three hundred miles east of the Chagos Archipelago an explosion took place, but whether external or internal the survivors did not know. One of them thought it might have been a mine. But it was severe enough to sink the *Hilda P. Murchison* in less than five minutes, and the sole survivors were the first mate and six hands of the duty watch, who managed to scramble into the only boat that had not been shattered.

Without food and with only a small barrico of water, they set off to make their way back to Australia, knowing that with the prevailing winds they stood a much better chance of making land there than if they attempted a three-hundred-mile beat to windward, with the risk of missing the Chagos Archipelago altogether.

That was eight days ago. They contrived to exist upon raw fish, tallow candles—which they found in a locker—and half a pint of water per man per diem.

Once they sighted a vessel, but their signals for assistance were unnoticed. Then they encountered a white squall, the tail end of a storm that ripped their sails before they could stow canvas and carried away the rudder.

The blow was succeeded by a flat calm. For hours the cutter drifted idly, her roughly repaired sails hanging listlessly in the sultry air. Almost overcome by hunger, fatigue, and the tropical heat, they were on the point of despair when the timely arrival of the British airship snatched them from a lingering death.

"I hope we'll be able to set you ashore at Fremantle within the next eight or ten hours," said Fosterdyke. "Meanwhile we'll get in touch with the wireless station there and report your rescue. Oh, yes, you may smoke in the for'ard compartment, but you'll find this ship as 'dry' as the land of the Stars and Stripes."

During the rest of the day progress was well maintained. The westerly breeze increased to half a gale, which meant an addition of thirty to forty miles an hour to the airship's speed. Barring accidents the *Golden Hind* would reach Fremantle with petrol still remaining in her tanks.

"It's not often one gets a westerly wind in the Twenties," observed the baronet. "South-east Trades are the usual order of things. We're lucky. Normally we should have to go as far south as 40° to rely upon a westerly wind."

"It will help us from Fremantle to New Zealand," said Peter. "I remember reading in the paper not so many months ago of the skipper of a sailing vessel who tried for days to beat up from Melbourne to Fremantle. Finally, he gave up beating to wind'ard as a hopeless job, so he turned and ran before the westerly breeze, sailed round the Horn and the Cape of Good Hope, and actually arrived at Fremantle several days before another vessel that had left Melbourne at the same time as he did."

"Let's hope we'll find an equally favouring wind to help us across the Pacific," remarked Fosterdyke. "We'll want it."

CHAPTER XV
REVELATIONS

"LAND AHEAD!"

The hail brought Fosterdyke and Bramsdean from their cabins with the utmost alacrity. They had not expected to sight Australia for another hour and a half, and now there was certainly land far away to the east'ard.

During the last three hours the clear sky had given place to a thick bank of dark clouds. Observations to determine the *Golden Hind*'s position were therefore out of the question. She was steering a compass course with the wind almost dead aft. It was a case of dead reckoning, and now no one knew exactly what part of Western Australia they were approaching—whether it was north or south of the Fremantle aerodrome.

"We'll do it before dark," declared Fosterdyke, confidently.

He had hardly spoken when Murgatroyd's head and shoulders appeared through the hatchway of the navigation room.

"We're on the last few gallons of petrol, sir," he reported. "I've me doubts if the engines'll run another ten minutes. They're slowing down now," he added.

"Switch off all but numbers 1 and 2 motors," ordered the baronet. "Keep these running for twenty minutes if you can, and we'll manage it."

But before the chief engineer could regain the for'ard motor-room the six aerial propellers were motionless. The *Golden Hind* no longer drove through the air, but simply drifted broadside on to the strong breeze.

Just as the sun sank in the Indian Ocean the airship crossed the coastline. Ten miles to the north could be discerned Perth and Fremantle—ten miles that, as far as the *Golden Hind* was concerned might have been a thousand.

"Down with her," ordered Fosterdyke. "Stand by with both grapnels. We'll have to trust to luck to find a good anchoring-ground."

It was not until the airship had passed over the railway running southward from Perth to Busselton that Kenyon noted a hill that might afford shelter from the strong wind.

Rapidly several thousand cubic feet of brodium were exhausted from the ballonets, with the result that the *Golden Hind* dropped to within a hundred feet of the ground.

There was just sufficient twilight to make out the nature of the landing place. It was a wide belt of grassland, dotted here and there with small trees. Hedges there were none.

"There are a couple of men on horseback, sir," reported Frampton.

"Good," replied Fosterdyke. "Let go both grapnels. See how she takes that."

Both of the stout barbed hooks engaged the moment they touched the ground. Even though the wire ropes were paid out in order to reduce the strain, the jerk was severe. Round swung the giant airship head to wind, but still she dragged. The grapnels had caught in a wire fence, and having uprooted half a dozen posts, were doing their level best to remove a five-mile sheep fence.

Up galloped the two farmers. The uprooting of their boundary fence hardly troubled them. The arrival of the airship—the first they had ever seen—occupied all their attention.

"Make fast for us, please," hailed Fosterdyke, having ordered another rope to be lowered.

"Right-o," was the reply. "We'll fix you up."

Dismounting and tethering their somewhat restive horses, the two Australians took the end of the third wire rope to the trunk of a large tree—the only one for miles, as it so happened. Fortunately, they knew how to make a rope fast—an accomplishment that few people other than seamen possess.

"Where are we?" asked the baronet.

"In Minto County, ten miles from Kelmscott," was the reply.

"Any petrol to be had hereabouts?"

"Sure," was the unexpected answer. "How much do you want?"

"A hundred gallons—enough to take us to Fremantle," replied Fosterdyke rather dubiously.

"Two hundred if you want," offered the good Samaritan. "I'll run it along in less than an hour."

"Will tomorrow at daybreak do equally as well?" asked Sir Reginald, knowing the difficulty and possible danger of handling quantities of the highly volatile spirit in the dark. "We'll be all right here until morning if the wind doesn't increase."

"It won't," declared the farmer, confidently. "If anything, it'll fall light. If you're in a hurry, I'll hitch you on to my motor lorry and tow you into Fremantle."

Fosterdyke thanked him and begged to be excused on the score that he was obliged by the terms of the race to make a flight without outside assistance in the matter of propulsion.

The two Australians, declining an invitation to go on board the airship, rode away in the darkness.

As the farmer had predicted, the wind fell away to a dead calm, so the airship was able to rest upon the ground, but ready, should the breeze spring up, to ascend to a hundred feet and there ride it out until the promised petrol was forthcoming.

"Now for our first dinner on or over Australian soil," exclaimed Fosterdyke. "By Jove, I'm hungry! What's going?"

He scanned the menu card. The cooks on the airship were good men at their work, and dinner, whenever circumstances permitted, was rather a formal affair.

"Hullo!" exclaimed Peter. "Covers laid for four, eh?"

"Yes," replied the baronet. "I'm expecting a guest. Ah! here he is. Let me introduce you to my friend, Mr. Trefusis."

Kenyon and Bramsdean could hardly conceal their astonishment, for standing just inside the doorway, immaculately dressed in well-cut clothes, was the man they had hitherto known as Otto Freising, the fellow who had attempted to shoot Fosterdyke at Alexandria.

"Secret Service," explained the baronet. "Had to keep the affair dark, even from you two fellows."

"You certainly did us in the eye," said Peter.

"No more than I did Señor Jaures," rejoined Trefusis. "I had a rotten time cooped up with that bird, but it was worth it."

"So, you've succeeded?" asked Fosterdyke.

Trefusis nodded.

"Wouldn't be here if I hadn't," he remarked. "It took me some time to get the right side of Señor Enrico, but I managed it. He rather looked a bit sideways at me when I pitched a yarn about being a Hun. However, I've got it out of him that he was employed by von Sinzig to kipper your part of the show, and judging by accounts he almost succeeded. You'll have enough evidence, Fosterdyke, to disqualify von Sinzig."

"I'll think about it," drawled the baronet. "After all's said and done the Hun is a sport, only his idea of sport differs radically from ours. It's his nature, I suppose. But another time you fire at me with blank cartridges, Trefusis, old son, please don't aim at my head. Grains of burnt powder in one's eyes aren't pleasant."

"Nor did I feel very pleasant," rejoined the Secret Service man, "when that officious blighter suggested putting me under arrest and trying me in a Civil Court. He must have thought you pretty high-handed, rushing me off in your airship."

"Yes, it was as well I took Colonel Holmes into my confidence," said Fosterdyke. "Otherwise you might at this moment be cooling your heels in a 'Gippy' prison. However, we've got evidence against von Sinzig, if needs be."

"What are you going to do with Señor Jaures?" asked Trefusis.

"Do with him? Nothing much. Fact, I'll do it now, directly we've finished dinner."

The meal over, Fosterdyke ordered Enrico Jaures to be brought in. The look on the miscreant's features was positively astounding when he found his former companion in captivity revealed in his true colours.

"Now, Enrico Jaures," began Fosterdyke, without further preliminaries. "You understand English, in spite of your previous denial. Read that. If you agree to it, you are a free man the moment you've signed the statement."

At the promise of liberty Enrico plucked up courage. He had a wholesome respect for the word of an Englishman.

The document was in the form of a confession, stating that Enrico Jaures had agreed, for a certain sum promised by Count Karl von Sinzig, to hinder, either by crippling or destroying the *Golden Hind*, Sir Reginald Fosterdyke's attempt to fly round the world.

"I'll sign," said Enrico.

He wrote his name. Kenyon and Trefusis witnessed the signature.

The baronet folded the document and placed it in his pocket.

"Now you can go," he said.

"But how am I to return to Gibraltar?" asked Jaures.

"That's your affair," replied Fosterdyke, sternly. "You ought to be thankful you're still alive. Now go."

At the first sign of dawn the Australian farmer, true to his word, arrived with a large lorry piled with filled petrol cans. He was not alone. The seemingly sparsely populated district now teemed with people. Hundreds must have seen the *Golden Hind* pass overhead the previous evening, but how they discovered the airship's temporary anchorage was a mystery. There were townsmen in motorcars, sturdy farmers on motorcycles, waggons, and carts, backwoodsmen on bicycles and on foot. Even the "sun-downer" class were represented.

The *Golden Hind* had just completed her preparations for flying back to Fremantle aerodrome when a motorcyclist rode up and handed Fosterdyke a telegram.

"It was fortunate we didn't make Fremantle last night," observed the baronet, handing the message to Kenyon and Bramsdean. "The aerodrome was destroyed by fire at one o'clock this morning."

CHAPTER XVI
THE OBSERVATION BASKET

WHILE THE *GOLDEN HIND* was struggling towards the shores of Western Australia, Count Karl von Sinzig in *Z64* was flying almost due south from Samarang, in the island of Java.

He, too, had had a taste of the cyclone, which had extended over the whole of the Arabian Sea and had been severely felt as far north as the Persian-Turkestan frontier.

Practically helpless in the grip of the furious blast, *Z64* had been driven far off her course. Passing high over the mountainous districts of Thibet, the German airship, unseen and unheard, finally encountered a stiff northerly wind when approaching the China Sea in the neighbourhood of Hanoi. Already the start von Sinzig had obtained over his British rival was wiped out. The long detour he had been obliged to take represented twelve hours' flight under normal conditions, and since he knew of Fosterdyke's progress by the expedient of picking up the *Golden Hind*'s wireless message, he realised that the latter had made good her belated departure.

At Samarang, *Z64* took in fresh hydrogen and petrol. Von Sinzig reported his arrival to the representatives of the International Air Board, and stated his intention of proceeding via New Guinea, New Caledonia, and Norfolk Island to New Zealand, where he would be able to fulfil one of the conditions that required the competitors to touch at a spot within one degree of the nadir to their starting point.

But von Sinzig had no intention of carrying out his declared programme. Directly he was well clear of Samarang, he shaped a course due south in order to pick up the prevailing westerly wind south of Australia on which Fosterdyke counted also. A stiff northerly wind over the Sunda Sea helped the German to attain his object, and on the evening that the *Golden Hind* drifted to south of Fremantle, *Z64* was skirting the coast of West Australia, in the neighbourhood of Geographe Bay.

Von Sinzig was in a bad state of mind. He knew by means of a code message from Barcelona that one of his agents had made an attempt to delay the *Golden Hind*'s departure. What had actually taken place he knew not. All he did know was the galling fact that the attempt had been unsuccessful, and that by this time his rival was practically level with him.

"Hans," he exclaimed, calling one of his subordinates, formerly an Unter-Leutnant in the German Flying Service and before that a Mercantile Marine officer.

Hans Leutter clicked his heels and stood to attention.

"You know Fremantle?" asked the count, brusquely.

"Fairly well, mein Herr," was the reply. "I've called there perhaps a dozen times in cargo boats. The last time was in January, 1914."

"There was, of course, no aerodrome there then?"

"Assuredly no, sir."

"According to my information it is on the right bank of the Swan River and a couple of kilometres to the east of the town. It ought to be easily found."

Hans Leutter agreed that to locate it ought to be a simple matter.

"Then we'll do so, little Hans," exclaimed the count, grimly. "We might even make the Englishman Fosterdyke a little present anonymously, of course."

The ex-Unter-Leutnant grinned.

"You wish me to take the *Albatross* for an airing then?" he said.

"Ach, no," replied von Sinzig. "If our *Albatross* were invisible and noiseless, it would be different. We'll use the observation basket. Overhaul the mechanism carefully, because you, little Hans, are going to use it."

Hans Leutter saluted and went for'ard. He was not at all keen on being told off for observation work, but his innate sense of discipline made him accept the duty without outward signs of resentment. Somehow he didn't relish the idea of being lowered from the Zeppelin and allowed to dangle at the end of two or three thousand feet of fine wire.

Shortly before midnight the look-out on Z64 picked up the harbour and town lights of Fremantle. It was now a fairly calm night. At five thousand feet was a stratum of light clouds, sufficient to obscure the starlight. The climatic conditions for von Sinzig's plans were exactly what he wanted.

When the German airship was dead to windward of the town her motors were switched off and she was allowed to drift in and out of the lower edge of the bank of clouds.

From her foremost nacelle a circular basket, fitted with a vertical vane to prevent it from turning round and round like a gigantic meat-jack, was hanging. In the basket, with a couple of small incendiary bombs for company, was Hans Leutter. In order to keep in touch with the captain of Z64 Hans was provided with a wireless telephone.

"All ready," announced the observer. "Lower away."

The well-oiled mechanism ran smoothly and noiselessly until a sudden check in the downward journey told Hans that the observation basket had reached the limit of its cable. From where he dangled—nearly two-thirds of a mile below the airship—Z64 was quite invisible. It was therefore safe to assume that the good people of Fremantle were likewise not in a position to see the huge gas-bag five thousand feet overhead, while the insignificant observation basket, although only a thousand feet or so up, was too minute to be spotted against the blurred starlight.

On the other hand, Hans Leutter could command a fairly comprehensive view of the town beneath him. The tranquil waters of the Swan River enabled him to fix his position, for even on the darkest night a river can readily be seen by an aerial observer. The navigation lamps of the aerodrome almost misled him. At first he mistook them for the railway station; but when he discovered his mistake he asked himself why the aerial signalling lamps were still being exhibited. According to the latest wireless messages picked up by Z64, the *Golden Hind* ought by this time to be berthed in the hangar. But, perhaps, he argued, the officials in their demonstrations of welcome had forgotten to switch the lights off.

"This reminds me of London in 1916," thought Hans. "London in those good old days when our Zeppelins came and went almost without let or hindrance. Now, my beauty, you and I must part."

He raised the bomb and poised it on the edge of the basket. In his excitement he had completely forgotten his fears at being suspended by a steel rope almost the same gauge as a piano-wire.

The incendiary bomb was quite a small affair, but none the less efficacious. In order to guard against identification should any of the metal parts be found, the vanes were stamped with the British Government marks, which showed that von Sinzig, with characteristic Teutonic thoroughness, had taken the precaution of covering his tracks. The British Air Ministry and the Australian Commonwealth Government could appraise responsibility later—by that time Z64 would be thousands of miles away.

Allowing for the slight breeze, Hans Leutter telephoned for the Zeppelin to steer ten degrees to the nor'ard. Slowly Z64 carried out the instructions, and seesawing gently the observation basket moved in a slightly different direction from its previous line of drift until the crucial moment arrived.

Hans Leutter released the bomb. For three seconds the observer could follow its downward passage; then it vanished into the darkness. Five seconds later the missile hit its objective.

There was no need for a second bomb. The airship shed was blazing fiercely.

The Hun in the basket spoke into the telephone.

"Direct hit," he reported. "Haul me up."

Z64 had once more stopped her motors and was rising rapidly above the bank of clouds. At the same time a motor winch was winding in the cable, and Hans Leutter's rate of progress as the basket whirred through the air brought back all his fears concerning his hazardous position. What if there were a flaw in the wire? It was ex-Government stuff, he recalled—material that might have been left lying in a neglected condition for months before von Sinzig acquired it for its present purpose. And supposing the wire slipped off the drum and got nipped in the cogs of the winch? A score of thoughts of a similar nature flashed across the observer's mind. He broke into a gentle perspiration. He trembled violently as a mental vision of himself hurtling through space gripped him in all its hideousness.

But the wire held. Hans Leutter was assisted into the nacelle, where he promptly fainted. By that time Z64 was several miles away from Fremantle, but a dull red glare on the horizon unmistakably indicated the extent of the conflagration.

Throughout the night Z64 flew at an altitude of not less than fifteen thousand feet. Dawn found her far to the south'ard of the Great Australian Bight.

Von Sinzig had good cause for keeping out of the beaten steamer tracks; nor did he intend to pass within a hundred miles of the southern part of Tasmania. He counted upon arriving at Napier, New Zealand, at daybreak on the day following, and until then he meant to be most careful not to be reported by any vessel.

The commander of Z64 had just sat down to breakfast when one of the crew entered his cabin.

"Pardon, Herr Offizier," said the man, apologetically, "but the observation basket is missing."

"What do you mean?" demanded von Sinzig.

"We secured it after Herr Leutter had finished with it, Herr Kapitan," explained the man. "I myself saw that the four bottle-screws were turned up tightly. Kaspar Graus, who had been told to remove the remaining petrol bomb, came and reported that the basket was no longer there. The metal clips were still attached to the bottle-screws. It would appear that these were torn from the basket itself."

Count Karl von Sinzig left his breakfast untasted and hurried along the catwalk to the gondola from which the observation basket was hung. His informant's news was only too true. Unaccountably the basket had been wrenched from its securing apparatus.

"It is of little consequence," he declared. "We would not have required it again, and, since it will not float, it is at the bottom of the sea by this time.

Perhaps it is as well, in case we are inspected by inquisitive officials at our next alighting place."

It was an unlucky day for Z64. About noon two of her motors developed trouble simultaneously. Three hours elapsed before the sweating mechanics were able to get the recalcitrant engines in running order again, and during that period the Zeppelin had perforce to slow down considerably. Consequently, it was half an hour after sunrise when Z64 sighted the Three Kings Island to the north-west of Cape Maria van Diemen. Here she altered course, so as ostensibly to appear as if she had been flying straight from New Caledonia, and, skirting the west coast of New Zealand, headed for Napier, where, by the consent of the New Zealand Government, von Sinzig was permitted to land and thus carry out one of the conditions of the contest.

"We'll fly inland when we sight Auckland," decided the count. "No, don't take her up any higher. There is now no need for concealment. Let these New Zealanders see and comment upon the fact that their islands are not beyond reach of a good German airship."

And so, flaunting her prowess in the rapidly growing daylight, Z64 approached the town of Auckland. The Zeppelin was within ten miles of the place when one of the crew shouted the disconcerting information that there was an airship on the starboard bow, travelling east by north.

Rapping out a furious oath, von Sinzig snatched up a pair of binoculars. He had never before set eyes on the *Golden Hind,* although the British airship had passed almost immediately above him within a few minutes of Z64 leaving her Spanish base, but instinctively he realised that this was his greatest rival, Sir Reginald Fosterdyke's creation.

"Gott in Himmel!" shouted von Sinzig. "Leutter, you numbskull, you made a hideous mess of things last night! Look—the *Golden Hind!*"

CHAPTER XVII
A SURPRISE FOR CAPTAIN PROUT

CAPTAIN ABRAHAM PROUT, MASTER and part owner of the topsail schooner *Myrtle*, of 120 tons burthen, came on deck on hearing the mate give the order "All hands shorten sail!"

It was six o'clock in the morning, still dark and very cold, for the *Myrtle* was on the fortieth parallel of the Southern Hemisphere, and the month being June it was mid-winter. There were flakes of snow flying about. For the last three days and nights it had either been sleeting, raining, or snowing, or else all three together; but the wind was fair, and there was every prospect of the schooner making a quick passage from Albany to Hobart.

"There's something behind this muck, Abe," remarked the mate, who, on the strength of being the "Old Man's" brother-in-law, was on familiar terms with Captain Prout. "The old hooker won't carry her topsails with the breeze a-freshenin'. Best be on the safe side, says I."

"Quite right, Tom," agreed the skipper. "New topmasts cost a mort sight o' money in these hard times. Anything to report?"

"Nothin'," replied the mate, laconically.

He shook the frozen sleet from the rim of his sou'wester and turned to inform one of the crew, in polite language of the sea, that "he'd better get a move on an' not stand there a-hanging on to the slack."

"There's some tea a-goin', Tom," announced Captain Prout. "Nip below an' get a mug to warm you up a bit."

The mate fell in with the suggestion with alacrity. The skipper, having seen the hands complete their task of "gettin' the tops'ls off her," went aft to where the half-frozen helmsman was almost mechanically toying with the wheel.

Through sheer force of habit Captain Prout peered into the feebly illuminated compass-bowl. Even as he did so, there was a tremendous crash.

The *Myrtle* trembled from truck to kelson, while from aloft a jumble of splintered spars, cordage, and canvas fell upon the deck like a miniature avalanche.

Captain Prout's first impressions were those of pained surprise. For the moment he was firmly convinced that the schooner had piled herself upon an uncharted rock, but the absence of any signs of the vessel pounding against a hard bottom reassured him on that point.

Although in ignorance of what had occurred, the tough old skipper rose to the occasion.

"Steady on your helm!" he shouted to the man at the wheel. "Don't let her fall off her course."

The helmsman obeyed. It was no easy matter, since he was enveloped in a fold of the mainsail and the *Myrtle* was towing the main-topmast and a portion of the cross-trees alongside.

Alarmed by the commotion, the "watch below"—two men and a boy—rushed on deck, while the mate, issuing from the after-cabin with a tin pannikin of tea still grasped in his hand, raised his voice in a strongly worded enquiry to know what had happened to the old hooker.

"Get a light, Tom, an' we'll have a squint at the damage," shouted the Old Man. "One of you sound the well and see if she's making any. Dick, you just see if them sidelights are burning properly."

The mate disappeared, to return with a hurricane lamp.

"Jerusalem!" he exclaimed. "Ain't it a lash up?"

The mainmast had been broken off five feet below the cross-trees, with the result that the main and throat halliard blocks had gone with the broken spars, while the mainsail, with the gaff and boom, had fallen across the deck. The shroud halliards still held, and the wire shrouds themselves trailed athwart both bulwarks. Apparently the foremast was intact, since it was the main topmast stay that had parted under the strain.

This much Captain Prout saw, noted, and understood, but what puzzled him was a telescoped object, looking very much like an exaggerated top-hat, that lay upon the deck between the mainmast fife-rail and the coaming of the main hatch.

"Guess it's a meteorite," hazarded the mate.

"Meteorite, my foot!" said Captain Prout, scornfully. "If't had been, 'twould ha' gone slap bang through the old hooker, an' we'd have been in the ditch."

"It's had a good try, anyway," rejoined the mate. "Half a dozen deck planks stove in."

He held the lantern close to the mysterious object.

"Looks like a bloomin' bath," he continued, "and I'm hanged if there isn't a whopping big bird in it. Rummiest birdcage I've ever set eyes on."

The cause of the damage to the *Myrtle's* top-hamper and deck planks was Z64's observation basket. Instead of falling into the sea and decorously sinking to the bottom, as von Sinzig had hoped, the contrivance had struck the only vessel within a radius of a hundred miles. With its head and neck driven completely through the aluminium side of the basket was a large eagle. The huge bird had struck the suspended basket with such a tremendous blow that the impact had wrenched away the metal clips securing it to the bottle-screws.

"Standin' an' looking at the blessed thing won't clear away this raffle," said the Old Man with asperity. "Set to, all hands. Secure and belay all you can and cut the rest adrift."

"Heave this lot overboard, Abe?" questioned the mate, kicking the basket with his sea-boot.

"Best let 'un stop awhile," decided the skipper. "Pass a lashing round it. Be sharp with that topmast, or it'll stove us in."

Quickly the mate and a couple of hands cut away the rigging that held the topmast alongside. The heavy spar, which had been bumping heavily against the side, fell clear. The *Myrtle*, no longer impeded by the trailing wreckage, forged rapidly through the water, although she was now carrying foresail, staysail, and outer jib only.

By this time day had broken. The snow had ceased falling, and right ahead the pale sun shone in a grey, misty sky.

The crew, having made all ship-shape as far as lay in their power, were curiously regarding the cause of the catastrophe. They rather looked upon it as a diversion to break the monotony.

"There's a log of sorts, sir," exclaimed one of the men, fumbling with the leather straps that secured the unused petrol bomb. The missile had been badly dented, but luckily the safety cap was intact. Had it not been so, the bomb would have ignited on impact, and the *Myrtle*, her snow-swept deck notwithstanding, would soon have been enveloped in flames from stem to stern.

"Don't fool around with it, Ted," said another of the crew, who, an R.N.R. man, had seen life and death in the Great War. "It's a bomb."

"Well," observed Captain Prout, "that's more'n I bargained for. I've taken my chances with floating mines, but it's coming too much of a good thing when these airmen blokes start chucking bombs haphazard-like."

"Best pitch the thing overboard," suggested the mate.

"No," objected the Old Man. "If we do, we've no evidence. Someone's got to pay for this lash up. Government broad arrow on the thing, too. That fixes it. When we make Hobart I'll raise Cain or my name's not Abraham Prout."

CHAPTER XVIII
UNDER FIRE

"IT'S GOING TO BE a close race, Kenyon," remarked Fosterdyke, as Z64 crossed the *Golden Hind*'s bows at a distance of less than a mile.

"Guess we're top-dog, though," replied Kenneth. "We've wiped out the Hun's useful lead, and at the half-way point we're practically level."

"Yes," agreed the baronet; "but we must not ignore the element of chance. Let me see"—he referred to the large Mercator map—"according to the latest reports, Commodore Nye's 'Eagle' is at Khartoum. His hop across the Atlantic and a non-stop run over the Sahara takes a lot of beating. I'd like to meet that Yankee. And there's the Jap, Count Hyashi. He's at Panama, after having been hung up for three days at Honolulu. If he'd been able to carry on without a hitch, his quadruplane would have won the race. So it appears that all the competitors have completed half the course at practically the same time."

"Airplane approaching, sir," reported Collings.

Right ahead a biplane was heading towards the *Golden Hind*, followed at close intervals by three more. Seemingly ignoring the German airship, which was now on a diverging course, the four machines with admirable precision turned and accompanied the British airship.

Two took up station on either side of the *Golden Hind*. Each flew the New Zealand ensign. It was Fosterdyke's preliminary welcome to the Antipodes.

Gliding serenely earthwards in perfectly calm air, the *Golden Hind* entered the big shed prepared for her reception. The civic officials of Auckland turned out in force, supported by crowds of "Diggers" and a fair sprinkling of Maoris.

"We quite understand," was the mayor's remark when Fosterdyke, thanking him for the warmness of his reception, firmly but courteously refused to attend a banquet proposed to be given in his honour. "This is a race, not a ceremonial tour. The prestige of the Empire is at stake, so get on with it."

Accordingly, the *Golden Hind*'s crew did "get on with it." Aided by scores of willing helpers, they replenished fuel tanks, took in fresh water and provisions and necessary stores. A representative of the International Air Board was in attendance to sign the control sheet, certifying that the *Golden Hind* had completed half the circuit, and had touched at a spot within a degree of the opposite point of the globe to his starting point. Within an hour and a quarter of her arrival at Auckland the British airship started on her homeward voyage.

Although New Zealand had no cause to show any goodwill towards the Huns, von Sinzig had no reason to complain of his reception. He was received coldly, it is true, but the New Zealanders, sportsmen all, were not ones to put obstacles in the way of an alien and former enemy.

Notified by wireless of Z64's impending arrival at Napier, the authorities at that town had cylinders of hydrogen and a large stock of petrol in readiness for the German airship's requirements. Within ten minutes of the *Golden Hind*'s departure from Auckland Z64 started from Napier.

The contest had now entered a more interesting phase. It was almost certain that the rivals would take a practically identical course, crossing the American continent in the neighbourhood of the Isthmus of Panama. The lofty Andes, extending like a gigantic backbone from Colombia to Patagonia—an almost uninterrupted range 450 miles in length—presented a difficult, though not exactly insurmountable obstacle to the rival airships.

Vainly the wireless operators of the *Golden Hind* sought to "pick up" the Zeppelin. Von Sinzig had seen to that, for directly the German airship left New Zealand he gave orders that on no account were messages to be transmitted, but on the other hand, the receivers were to be constantly in use, in order to pick up any radiograms that might throw light upon the movements of the *Golden Hind*.

Apart from the chagrin at the knowledge that his attempt to burn the British airship was a failure, von Sinzig felt rather elated. His deceptive report of the course he had taken from Java to New Zealand had been accepted by the authorities without question; hence no suspicion could possibly be attached to him for the burning of the Fremantle aerodrome. He was also of the opinion that Z64 was a swifter craft than her rival and possessed another advantage—that of greater fuel-carrying capacity. Even if the *Golden Hind* did possess a higher speed, she would have to alight more frequently to replenish her tanks.

As far as the *Golden Hind* was concerned the run across the Panama was almost devoid of incident. With the exception of a distant view of Pitcairn Island—famous in connection with the mutiny of the *Bounty*—no land was sighted until Galapagos Group was seen ten miles on the starboard bow.

The *Golden Hind* was now re-crossing the equator. Fosterdyke, who had crossed the line at least a dozen times, in all sorts of vessels from luxuriant liners to singy tramps, and even on one occasion on board a wind-jammer, declared that there was nothing to beat an airship for travelling in the Tropics.

"For one thing you can keep cool," he added; "another, that will appeal to a good many people, is the fact that an airship is beyond reach of Father Neptune and his merry myrmidons. And the Doldrums, instead of being regarded as a terror, afford an easy passage to aircraft of all descriptions."

With the setting of the sun a thick mist arose—one of those humid tropical mists that are responsible for malaria and other zymotic diseases peculiar to the Torrid Zone.

At a couple or three thousand feet altitude, the *Golden Hind* was in pure clear air, but in the brief twilight the banks of mist as viewed from above were picturesque in the extreme.

But to the crew of the *Golden Hind* the picturesqueness of the scene was in a measure unappreciated. They were nearing land, and a fog was one of the most undesirable climatic conditions. Not only was time a consideration, but the petrol supply was running low. But for this, Fosterdyke would have slowed down and cruised around until the mists dispersed with daybreak.

"We'll have to risk it and make a descent," he declared. "Anywhere within easy distance of Panama will do, because it is a calm night and there will be little or no risk of the *Golden Hind* being exposed to a high wind. Thank goodness we've directional wireless."

At length Fosterdyke felt convinced that the *Golden Hind* was nearing Panama. He had arranged by wireless to detonate three explosive rockets, and the United States Air Station was to reply with a similar signal, while searchlights, directed vertically, would enable the airship to locate the landing-ground.

"Hanged if I can see any searchlights," exclaimed Bramsdean.

"Killed by the mist," explained the baronet. "I fancy I see a blurr of light two points on our port bow. What's that, Truscott?"

The wireless operator had left his cabin and was standing behind Fosterdyke as the latter was peering through the darkness.

"There's a jam for some reason," announced Truscott. "For the last five minutes I've been calling up Panama, but there's nothin' doin'. A high-powered installation, using the same metre-wave, is cutting in. I asked them to knock off, but they haven't done so."

"Inconsiderate blighters!" exclaimed Fosterdyke. "Never mind, Truscott, we can get along all right now. I fancy I can see the aerodrome lights."

"Yes, sir," agreed Kenyon. "One point on our port bow now."

"Then fire the rockets," ordered the baronet, at the same time telegraphing for the motors to be declutched.

Three vivid flashes rent the darkness, their brilliance illuminating a wide area of the fog-bank a thousand feet below, while the report echoed over the level line of misty vapour like a continuous peal of thunder.

Within a minute of the discharge of the third rocket two bursts of flame, accompanied by sharp reports, occurred at a distance of less than a quarter of a mile of the *Golden Hind*'s port quarter, while after an interval of fifteen seconds three more exploded simultaneously in the same direction.

"Guess Uncle Sam can't count," remarked Kenyon, imitating to perfection the nasal drawl of the typical New Englander.

"Looks to me like shrapnel," added Bramsdean. "Judging by the way the smoke mushroomed, it reminds me of Archies over the Hun lines."

"Good enough, we'll drop gently," decided Fosterdyke. "Stand by with the holding-down lines and have a couple of grapnels ready."

The amount of brodium necessary to more than neutralise the lifting power of the gas and the dead weight of the airship was exhausted from the requisite number of ballonets, and the *Golden Hind* began to sink almost vertically in the still air.

Within five minutes she entered the belt of mist—a warm, sickly-smelling atmosphere that reminded Kenyon of a hot-house.

"I hear voices," announced Peter.

Not far beneath the airship men were shouting and talking excitedly, but the crew of the *Golden Hind* were unable to understand what the men were saying.

"Ahoy, there!" hailed Fosterdyke. "Stand by to take our ropes."

Both grapnels were carefully lowered, since there would be grave risks entailed by throwing them overboard. At the same time half a dozen holding-down ropes were paid out from each side of the nacelle. These were caught by unseen hands, and the airship was quickly drawn earthwards at far too great a speed to please Sir Reginald Fosterdyke.

"Gently," he shouted. "Avast heaving."

The response was a terrible surprise. Simultaneously two searchlights were unmasked, their powerful beams at short range punctuating the fog and impinging upon the enormous envelope of the *Golden Hind*, while an irregular fusillade of musketry assailed the airship on all sides.

"Up with her!" shouted Fosterdyke. "Charge all the ballonets. We've struck a revolution."

CHAPTER XIX
VICTIMS OF A REVOLUTION

ABOVE THE STACCATO OF rifle-firing rose the roar of the *Golden Hind*'s powerful motors. Volumes of brodium, released from the pressure-flasks, rushed into the ballonets. The airship rose at an oblique angle, her nose almost touching the ground. Then, as the aerial propellers went ahead, the fore-part of the fuselage ploughed over the rough ground.

With thirty or forty men hanging on like grim death to the guidelines, and as many more tailing on to the grapnel ropes, the *Golden Hind*, with gas leaking from numerous bullet holes in her ballonets, was unable to seek refuge in her natural element.

Fortunately for the safety of the airship's crew, the rifle-firing quickly ceased as soon as the attackers realised that they had effected her capture. Apparently it was their intention to prevent further damage being done to the huge airship.

Finding that escape was impossible and unable to offer resistance, Fosterdyke opened out one of the doors of the nacelle and raised his hands above his head. It was no disgrace in surrendering thus. Alive the crew of the *Golden Hind* could offer and receive explanations. Dead, they could not.

The appearance of the captain of the *Golden Hind* was greeted by peremptory orders, shouted in an unintelligible language. It certainly wasn't American. It seemed to Fosterdyke that it was a kind of Spanish, and since he was ignorant of that tongue he failed to grasp the meaning of the volume of directions.

Covered by scores of rifles, Fosterdyke, Kenyon, and Bramsdean headed the crew of the airship. Completely bewildered by the aggressive nature of their reception, and not knowing what fate would befall them, the position of the British airmen was critical in the extreme. Yet they bore themselves calmly and bravely, scorning to let their captors know that inwardly at least they "felt the breeze."

Deftly, as if they were well used to performing the operation, two half-breeds searched the baronet for concealed weapons. The rest of the crew were subjected to the same treatment. Finding nothing in the nature of arms, the searchers looked rather astonished and disappointed.

A gorgeously uniformed man, evidently the commandant of the band, walked up to the baronet and saluted with an elaborate flourish. There was little doubt about it; he had already come to the conclusion that a mistake had occurred, and that he rather feared the consequences.

"Americano, señor?" he asked.

"No," replied Fosterdyke. "English."

"Madre de Dios!" said the commandant in ill-concealed consternation. He shouted something to his followers. After a brief interval, a tall, olive-featured follower, whose black oiled locks fell on his shoulders, slouched forward and announced—

"Me speak English. Vot you do here?"

Mutual explanations took a considerable time; but eventually Fosterdyke and his companions gleaned the salient facts for the reason of the attack and capture of the *Golden Hind*.

In the tropical mists the airship had landed not in the Panama Zone but in a neighbouring republic, which, as is by no means an unusual occurrence, was indulging in a little political diversion in the shape of a revolution. Just at present there was no means of ascertaining which was the predominant faction, but one side had gained possession of an old airship—purchased at a disposal sale of one of the *Entente* countries. This airship, hastily fitted out and provided with bombs and machineguns, was known to be on the point of operating against the Federals. The latter were therefore expecting the raiding airship when the *Golden Hind*, miles out of her course owing to the mists and a side wind that, unknown to the navigating officers, had blown her well to leeward, fired her detonating rockets almost immediately over the Federal party's main force.

The Federals knew nothing of the Round the World Race; but their anxiety to make amends was most marked. They offered to provide unlimited supplies of petrol, and to render any assistance that lay in their power; but the fact remained that the hasty fusillade had caused considerable damage to the *Golden Hind*.

At first Fosterdyke thought that the airship was out of the running. Kenyon and Bramsdean were of the same opinion, for the loss of brodium through the punctured ballonets seemed a fatal obstacle to the immediate resumption of the flight.

Further examination revealed the fact that half the number of the ballonets were holed. Of these almost everyone could be patched and made gas-tight, since the rifle-bullets, being of small calibre and of high velocity, had bored minute holes. But what was far more serious was the shortage of brodium. Even by releasing the contents of the reserve cylinders it was doubtful whether there was sufficient to lift the airship.

"We'll have a good try, anyway," declared Fosterdyke. "Once we get her up we'll rely on our planes to get us across the Atlantic. Thank goodness the motors are intact! I wonder if there's much damage done to the navigation room. Several bullets came unpleasantly close to our heads, I remember."

Examination resulted in the knowledge that although the aluminium sides of the nacelle had been liberally peppered, most of the nickel bullets had penetrated both sides without doing vital damage. What was the most serious injury was caused to the propellers of Nos. 5 and 6 motors, the feather-edged blades being chipped by bullets. Since the spare blades had already been used earlier in the voyage replacement was out of the question. The ragged edges meant at least a reduction of ten miles an hour, even if the blades did not fly to pieces when the propellers were running at maximum speed.

During the rest of the night the crew worked with a will—patching, mending, and "doping" the holed fabric and carefully testing each repaired ballonet with compressed air before refilling it with the precious brodium.

Meanwhile, the Federals brought quantities of petrol, employing teams of mules for the purpose, their petrol dump being a good five miles from the scene of the *Golden Hind*'s unfortunate landing. Every drop had to be passed through a fine gauze strainer before being allowed to enter the tanks, since foreign matter in the fuel might easily result in motor trouble.

Anxious to make amends, the commandant also presented the baronet with a quantity of excellent tobacco and cigars, several native cakes made of maize, an earthenware bowl filled with good butter, and a wicker crate of fresh fruit.

By dawn the refitting of the *Golden Hind* was accomplished as far as lay in the power of the dauntless crew. Now came the crucial test: would the airship rise under the lifting power of the reduced volume of brodium?

At seven o'clock the huge fabric showed signs of buoyancy. A quarter of an hour later the recording instruments showed that only another thousand cubic feet of gas was necessary to overcome the force of gravity.

"We haven't that quantity, sir," reported Chief Air Mechanic Hayward. "But I would suggest, sir, that we release our reserve gas into the for'ard ballonets. That will lift her nose clear of the ground, and the propellers will do the rest. Once we're up, sir, it will be as easy as shelling peas."

"We can but try it," replied Fosterdyke. "At any rate, if we can make Panama we will manage with hydrogen for the remaining ballonets. Right-o! Pass the word when you're ready."

At seven-thirty the crew were at their stations. The for'ard portion of the airship was straining at the guide ropes. The declutched motors, purring gently at a quarter throttle, were awaiting the order that would transform them into propulsive forces. Until the planes could be brought into action the *Golden Hind* was much in the nature of a rocket soaring obliquely under the influence of a self-contained impulsive charge.

Throwing open one of the windows of the riddled navigation room, Foster-dyke surveyed the crowd below. The Federal troops, in spite of their bizarre uniforms and varied equipment, were fairly well disciplined. Those not actually engaged in holding down the airship were formed up at about fifty yards from the nacelle, interested spectators of the largest airship that had ever passed over the territory of the Central American Republic.

"Let go!" shouted the baronet.

The order, interpreted by the Creole who claimed to have a knowledge of English, was obeyed promptly. The men seemed to have an inkling of what would happen if they did not, and they dropped the guide ropes as though they were hot irons.

Simultaneously, as the bows of the *Golden Hind* lifted, Kenyon telegraphed for "full ahead."

With four of the propellers purring in their accustomed way and the two after ones roaring like gigantic buzzers, as the jagged edges revolved rapidly in the air, the *Golden Hind* ascended obliquely, with her major axis inclined at an angle of forty degrees to the horizontal.

The Federal troops were waving their nondescript headgear and brandishing their rifles in token of farewell. Doubtless they were cheering and shouting also, but the noise of the airship's propellers outvoiced all extraneous sounds.

At a height of one thousand feet the six planes were trimmed and brought into action, with the result that the *Golden Hind* settled down on almost an even keel.

Four minutes later the scene of the unfortunate "regrettable incident" was lost to sight.

"Thanks be, we're up!" said Fosterdyke.

CHAPTER XX
WIRELESS REPORTS

"KENYON!" EXCLAIMED THE BARONET.

"Sir?"

"We'll cut Panama," was Fosterdyke's astounding decision. "We'll carry straight away on. She's doing splendidly, shortage of brodium notwithstanding. We've plenty of fuel, so it's a dash for Madeira."

"How about reporting at the Panama control?" asked Kenneth.

"I'll risk omitting that," replied Sir Reginald. "Being mixed up in a potty revolution is quite sufficient excuse for non-compliance with regulations. It isn't as if we were bound to report ourselves, as in the case of Auckland. Bramsdean, you might ask the wireless operator to report us to Panama and enquire if there's any news of our rivals. Last night's affair has given von Sinzig a very useful lead, I'm afraid."

Peter hastened to give the necessary orders. Presently he returned.

"No news of the Hun, sir," he reported. "The Yankee airship made a bad landing at Port Denison, Queensland, and was totally destroyed by fire."

"Hard lines," remarked Fosterdyke, feelingly. "Commodore Nye is a good sport. I hope he wasn't injured?"

"Far from it," replied Bramsdean. "In fact he's reported to have cabled to Melbourne asking the Victorian Government if they can sell him a Vickers-Vimy, so that he can continue the contest."

"Good luck to him, then!" exclaimed the baronet. "And the Jap?"

"Looks like a winner, sir," replied Peter. "The quadruplane is reported passing over Calcutta."

"Next to beating Fritz myself, the Jap is the fellow I hope will do it," remarked Fosterdyke. "By Jove! I'd like to know where von Sinzig is and what he's doing."

The *Golden Hind*, now virtually a heavier-than-air machine, was doing her level best to make up for the unlucky contretemps that had delayed her for eight precious hours. Unaccountably the reduction of the volume of brodium in her ballonets, although the rigid aluminium envelope had not appreciably contracted, had resulted in a marked increase of speed. Judging by the time she took to cover the distance between Panama and Nevis, in the Lesser Antilles—a distance of 1250 miles—her speed over the water was not far short of 190 miles an hour.

"If those two props had not been crippled," lamented Kenyon, "we'd be doing a good two hundred."

"I'm content," rejoined Fosterdyke, "provided we can keep it up. If we don't lap Z64 in another twelve hours, you can jolly well boot me, Kenyon!"

A few minutes later the wireless operator appeared and handed Fosterdyke a long written message.

The baronet's face was a study of varying emotions as he read the news. Kenyon, watching him, wondered what had happened. Not that he was surprised; after the experiences of the last week or so, it would take something very much out of the common to take Kenneth Kenyon aback.

"Evidently our friend von Sinzig has butted in where he didn't ought," remarked Fosterdyke, handing his companion the slip of paper.

It was a general Marconigram communication to the Press Agency, and read as follows:

"Hobart, Tasmania, Thursday. The schooner *Myrtle*, Abraham Prout, master, arrived here this morning in a damaged condition. Her master reports that in lat. 43° 15' S., long. 141° 20' E., the schooner was hit by a falling object, which Captain Prout subsequently brought into port. Examination showed that the object in question was an airship observation box or basket. In it, fortunately intact, and with the safety vane locking the detonator-pin, was an incendiary bomb stamped with the broad arrow. Experts here agree that the bomb is certainly not a British Government's missile, and by certain markings on the observation basket it is safe to assume that it belonged to a German airship. The basket and the bomb are being forwarded to the Commonwealth Air Board Headquarters at Sydney."

Then came another report:

"Fremantle, Western Australia, Thursday. Investigations amongst the ruins of the aerodrome destroyed by fire yesterday morning have resulted in the finding of the remains of an aerial torpedo bearing the British Government mark. This discovery completely upsets the original theory as to the cause of the outbreak. Various rumours are afloat, but pending an official declaration on the subject, the Press is requested to confine reports to the actual known facts. A further communication will be made as soon as definite information is forthcoming."

"Yes, von Sinzig is getting desperate," remarked Kenyon. "It's a dead cert that he thought we were berthed in the Fremantle aerodrome that night. But how in the name of goodness did he get so far south? It was reported he went direct from Java to New Zealand, passing north of Australia."

"He reported, you mean," corrected Fosterdyke. "Trying to throw dust in one's eyes is an old trick of Fritz's. Personally, I don't believe he took the northern route, and that he picked up our wireless announcing our intention of making Fremantle, and then tried to do us in."

"He's done for himself, any old way," declared Kenyon. "I wonder if a Hun can ever be a sportsman?"

"I wonder," echoed the baronet. "I've come across a good many Huns during the last five years, but I'm hanged if I ever met one who knew how to play the game."

Half an hour later the *Golden Hind* intercepted a wireless message to the effect that the British, American, and French Governments had issued joint instructions for the German airship *Z64* to be detained at the next landing-place.

"That looks like business," commented Kenyon. "Von Sinzig's out of the running."

"Unless he contrives to land in Spanish territory," added the baronet. "There are the Canary Islands, for instance. He could, and probably will, claim immunity as a political offender. I don't think he can be extradited. You see, it has to be proved to the hilt that he actually and by deliberate intent dropped a bomb on the aerodrome. No, I fancy we haven't lost our Hun rival yet. He stands a chance of romping home, so it's up to us to beat *Z64*."

"I'd like to know what the blighter's doing now," said Kenneth, tentatively. "Perhaps he's within fifty miles of us."

"Provided he's fifty miles behind us, I won't worry my head about him," declared Sir Reginald. "I'm not particularly keen on coming in touch with him on a dark night. He might try his hand at another dirty trick."

CHAPTER XXI
VON SINZIG'S BID FOR SAFETY

Count Karl von Sinzig was in a particularly bad temper. He had just learned, by picking up various wireless messages, that "the cat was out of the bag." In other words, the discovery of the lost observation basket had landed him in a very awkward predicament.

He blamed everyone and everybody save himself. The luckless Unter-Leutnant, Hans Leutter, came in for a very bad time because he hadn't got rid of the second bomb. The petty officer, who had conscientiously seen that the bottle-screws securing the basket were properly made fast, was bullied and browbeaten because the basket was torn away. The rest of the crew, the makers of the airship, and every person having anything to do with the aerial contest also came in for abuse.

The count was also puzzled at not being able to intercept any messages from the *Golden Hind* after the one announcing her approach to Panama. *Z64* had reported at Colon, when, according to the latest information, the British airship was hard on the heels of her German rival.

And now, almost the final straw, came the general wireless message declaring that *Z64* was proscribed and liable to be detained should she touch at any place belonging to either of the *entente* nations.

Fosterdyke had accurately gauged his rival's intentions. The knowledge that his guilty secret was out compelled von Sinzig to change his plans and make for Teneriffe, whence, having replenished fuel, he ought to be easily able to complete the last stage of the round the world voyage.

When about 300 miles to the westward of the Canaries, but farther to the north than von Sinzig hoped to be, owing to a strong side-drift, *Z64* encountered a violent storm. In order to try to avoid the worst of the terrific wind and rain, the airship began to ascend, hoping to find better conditions in the rarefied atmosphere.

Z64 was ascending obliquely under the action of her huge horizontal rudders and was passing through a dense cloud when a vivid flash of lightning, followed almost immediately by a deafening crash of thunder, appeared to penetrate the airship through and through.

Almost every man on board shouted with terror. They were fully convinced that the hydrogen had ignited. There was a frantic rush for the life-saving parachutes, until Unter-Leutnant Hans Leutter reassured the panic-stricken crew with the information that the gas-bag had not taken fire.

Meanwhile the airship, left to its own devices, since the helmsman had abandoned the wheel, had turned eight degrees to port and was travelling at a rate of 120 miles an hour on a course N. by W.

Von Sinzig, who "had the wind up" as badly as anybody, was nowhere to be found for some time. Leutter even came to the conclusion that his superior officer had leapt overboard when the alarm of fire had been raised; but after a lapse of twenty-five minutes the count re-appeared, looking very grey and haggard.

"I think I must have been stunned, Herr Leutter," he said in explanation.

His subordinate accepted the excuse without smiling incredulously. He had seen his chief bolting for his very life. He certainly did not look like being stunned.

"Take charge for a while," continued von Sinzig. "I am not feeling well. I must go to my cabin and lie down."

He staggered aft along the narrow catwalk, while the Unter-Leutnant gave orders for the airship to be brought back on her original course.

It was easier said than done. The gigantic gas-bag was see-sawing erratically. She had difficulty in answering to her helm, and in spite of the fact that the horizontal rudders were trimmed for ascending, the airship was decreasing her altitude.

Then reports began to come in from the still "jumpy" crew. The engineer reported that the after propeller was damaged; another man announced that there was a large gash in the aluminium envelope, and that several of the after ballonets were leaking rapidly.

Further examination revealed the grave fact that one of the propeller blades had fractured, and the flying piece of metal had penetrated the gas-bag at about eighty feet from the after-end. So great had been the velocity of the broken blade that it had practically wrecked every gas compartment in the stern of the envelope.

Unter-Leutnant Leutter sent a man to inform von Sinzig. He had to do that, although he would have preferred to act upon his own initiative. He was decidedly "fed up" with his arrogant and craven skipper.

The count arrived quickly. He led off by abusing Leutter in front of several of the crew for having disturbed him; then, on being told of what had occurred, he changed completely round and complimented his subordinate on his sagacity.

"*Z64*'s done, Herr kapitan," declared Hans Leutter. "She's sinking rapidly. Half an hour, perhaps, will find her falling into the sea. We must take steps to safeguard ourselves."

"Quite true," agreed the count. "Although there will be enough buoyancy in the envelope to keep it afloat for hours—days even. What do you propose to do?"

"Throw overboard everything of a weighty nature, Herr kapitan," replied the Unter-Leutnant. "We can empty the petrol tanks, since we have no further use for the motors. Meanwhile we must send out a general wireless call for assistance to all ships within a hundred or two hundred kilometres of us."

Count Karl von Sinzig thought this quite an excellent idea. At least, he said so. At the back of his mind he had a hazy notion that even now there was a chance of winning the Chauvasse Prize. There was nothing in the conditions forbidding a competitor—

His ruminations were interrupted by the appearance of the wireless operator, who reported that both the transmitter and the receiver were out of action, and that the wireless cabin bore signs of having been struck by lightning.

"Can't you effect repairs?" demanded von Sinzig.

"I am sorry I cannot, Herr kapitan," replied the operator.

"A useful wireless man you are!" commented the count, caustically.

The man saluted and backed away from his chief, congratulating himself that he had come off so lightly. But von Sinzig was rather pleased than otherwise that the wireless was out of action. It furnished him with a good excuse to put a certain little plan into execution.

"Are there any vessels in sight?" he asked.

A look-out man had been scanning the wide expanse of sea for the last ten minutes.

"Nothing in sight, Herr kapitan," he announced.

By this time *Z64* was well beyond the storm area. The sea, now a bare 3000 feet below, was no longer white with angry crested waves, but by the aid of binoculars it could be seen that there was a long swell running.

"Then there's nothing to be done unless we make use of the *Albatross*," declared von Sinzig. "I will go and look for a ship."

Hans Leutter and those of the crew who heard the count's resolve received the proposal in stony silence. They all recognised that their kapitan was violating the traditions of the sea and the air by being the first to abandon his command. Of the crew at least four were capable of flying the small but powerful monoplane, so there was no excuse on that score of von Sinzig being the only man able to take the *Albatross* up.

In obedience to a peremptory order the crew hurriedly prepared the monoplane for her flight. The *Albatross*, nominally used for starting from and alighting on the ground, was adapted for marine work by having three small floats, the lower portions of which were just above the wheel base-line, so that the monoplane could be used either as an ordinary machine or as a seaplane.

In the present circumstances von Sinzig elected to start from the air. The *Albatross*, suspended by a quick release gear from the underside of the 'midship gondola, was ready before the airship had dropped to a thousand feet.

"You will be quite safe," reiterated the count. "I'll send the first vessel I meet to your assistance. It may be a matter of a few hours. All ready? Let go."

The monoplane's motor was already running slowly. Directly von Sinzig felt the *Albatross* had parted company with her gigantic parent he opened "all out." At a hundred and thirty miles an hour he was soon lost to sight.

"He's going east by north, I notice," soliloquised Hans Leutter. "I will be greatly surprised if he returns to Z64."

And the count was of the same opinion. He hadn't the faintest intention of flying back to the airship. Nor was he particularly keen on reporting Z64's predicament to any vessel he sighted.

He was out to win the Chauvasse Prize. The sum went to the man who succeeded in flying round the world in twenty days. There was no stipulation to the effect that only one airship, flying-boat, airplane, or seaplane must be used throughout the flight. Therefore, since the goal was within a comparatively easy distance, he hoped to complete the circuit in the *Albatross*, and thus win the coveted prize.

CHAPTER XXII
THE END OF Z64

"By Jove! Kenyon, what's that over on our starboard bow?" exclaimed Bramsdean.

Kenneth raised his binoculars and focussed them on a dark object in the direction indicated.

"That," he replied after a brief survey, "is a Zepp. There's not much mistake about that. She is also in difficulties apparently, since Zepps don't generally assume an angle of forty-five degrees. It is also reasonable to assume that it is Z64, since we know that von Sinzig was keeping a course slightly divergent to ours. The southerly wind has evidently driven her northward."

Fosterdyke was asleep in his cabin, but upon hearing the news he hurried to the navigation room.

"Are we Pharisees or Good Samaritans, sir?" asked Kenyon. "Do we pass by on the other side, or do we stop to render assistance?"

"It strikes me that something more than assistance is required," replied the baronet. "Obviously our friend von Sinzig is out of the running. His airship is down and out. If there are any of the crew on board, we'll be just in time to prevent them losing the number of their mess."

Z64 was in a very bad way. The after part of the envelope was half submerged. The rearmost gondola was entirely so. The foremost car was rising and falling owing to the slight buoyancy of the for'ard ballonets. At one moment it was thirty or forty feet above the water, at another it was smacking the surface and sending the spray far and wide.

"Keep to windward," ordered Fosterdyke.

"There are men still on board," replied Peter. "A dozen more or less are hanging on to the catwalk."

"It'll be rather a proposition to get them off," said the baronet. "We haven't a boat; neither apparently have they, and I don't like the idea of running alongside a half-submerged gas-bag. With this heavy swell there's no knowing what might happen."

"We might run out a hawser and take her in tow," suggested Kenyon. "I mean, tow her until we get the crew off by means of an endless line."

"Might do," half agreed Fosterdyke. "It would be decidedly awkward if our head fell away and we drifted in broadside on to the wreckage. We'll try it. Tell Jackson to get a hawser ready, and see there is a slip fitted in case we have to cast off in a hurry."

Already several of the ballonets that at first sight seemed beyond repair had been patched up, while the fortunate discovery of two flasks of compressed brodium gave the *Golden Hind* considerable buoyancy, so that she was no longer dependent upon the lift of her six planes. Yet the prospect of having to take on board the weighty Hun crew would seriously threaten the buoyancy of the airship.

"Luckily we are within sight of our goal," said Fosterdyke. "We can sacrifice a quantity of our stores. The reserve freshwater tank can be started, too. Two hundred and fifty gallons less of water ought to make a considerable difference."

Leading Hand Jackson, with the help of four or five of the crew, soon made the necessary preparations. By this time the *Golden Hind* had approached to within a hundred yards of the disabled Zeppelin, the crew of which, half in doubt as to what was going to happen, were signalling and shouting frantically for help.

"Rescuing the crew of the *Hilda P. Murchison* was child's play to this," commented Kenyon. "Goodness only knows how we are going to establish communication. Her blessed envelope is in the way."

Thrice the *Golden Hind* sailed over her crippled rival. The trailing hawser glided over the rounded surface of the gasbag, but none of the men made any attempt to leave the gondolas and secure the rope. It afterwards transpired that the aluminium envelope was sagging and whipping to such an extent that the vertical shaft through it by which access could be made to the upper surface of the gas-bag was impracticable. Anyone attempting to ascend by that way would almost certainly be crushed to death.

"Can't the lubbers see the hawser?" asked Fosterdyke, impatiently. "Or have they all got the wind up so frightfully that they can't lift a hand to help themselves? Get in that hawser, Jackson. We'll try approaching to leeward this time and see if they've got the sense to veer a rope."

The manoeuvre required very careful execution. The *Golden Hind*, descending until her fuselage was but a few feet above the sea, approached carefully. She had to be kept under control up to a certain point, when way had to be taken off her. If she stopped too soon, she would drift away before communication could be established; if she carried on even a few yards too much, there was a danger of her overlapping envelope colliding nose on with the wrecked Zeppelin.

This time the Huns showed decided activity. They bent a line to an inflated India-rubber lifebelt and threw the latter into the sea. Unfortunately, they did not take into account the fact that the Zeppelin was drifting to leeward as fast as the lifebelt. When they realised what was happening one of the crew jumped overboard and towed the line a hundred yards or so away.

"Now there's a chance of doing something," commented Fosterdyke, telegraphing for a touch ahead with Nos. 1 and 2 motors.

As the *Golden Hind* passed immediately over the life-buoy a grapnel, lowered from the after-part of the fuselage, engaged the rope, and in a remarkably short space of time a stout hawser connected the British airship with the still buoyant bows of the German.

Fosterdyke waited until the *Golden Hind* had swung round and was pointing "down wind," then he ordered easy ahead with the two for'ard motors. This gave sufficient tension to the hawser, which was now inclined at an angle of about thirty degrees.

A "snatch-block" with an endless line was then allowed to run down to the hawser.

"Now the rest is easy," declared Fosterdyke, but for once at least he was greatly mistaken.

The first of the Huns arrived in a bowline on board the *Golden Hind*.

"How many are there?" asked Fosterdyke.

"Ve vos dwanty," replied the German, holding up the fingers of both hands twice in order to make his meaning clearer.

More Huns emerging from the for'ard gondola of Z64 confirmed the man's statement. One was evidently an officer, but his features did not in the least resemble those of Count von Sinzig, whose photograph had appeared some time back in the illustrated papers.

Seventeen Huns were transhipped in about as many minutes. The eighteenth was half-way along the tautened hawser when Fosterdyke shouted, "Let go!"

Leading-Hand Jackson obeyed the order instantly. The ring of the Senhouse slip was knocked clear, and the hawser fell with a splash into the sea. The *Golden Hind*, released from the drag of the partly water-logged Zeppelin, shot ahead.

She was only just in time. The baronet had noticed a tongue of flame issuing from the centre gondola of Z64. How the fire was caused was a mystery, since had the Huns wished to destroy the wreckage they would have waited until the last man was clear of the Zeppelin. Possibly the wiring of the electric stove had short-circuited when in contact with the salt water.

In less than fifteen seconds from the time the hawser had been slipped the hydrogen escaping from the leaky ballonets was ignited. The aluminium gasbag was surrounded by flames. The heat caused the gas in the still intact ballonets to expand, affording sufficient lifting power to heave the wreckage almost clear of the water. The remaining Huns, keenly alive to the terrible danger, promptly jumped into the sea.

Then with a terrific glare the remaining ballonets burst, and the shattered wreckage, sizzling as it came into contact with the cold water, disappeared beneath the surface, leaving a steadily widening circle of oil surmounted by a dense pall of black smoke to mark the scene of the end of Z64.

Before the evil-smelling vapour had dispersed the *Golden Hind*, turning head to wind, was over the spot searching for possible survivors. For half an hour she cruised round, but her efforts to rescue the three Huns were unavailing. The men had either been stunned by the explosion or had been hit by falling wreckage. Amongst them was Unter-Leutnant Hans Leutter, who, by resolutely refusing to leave his command until the rest of the crew were safe, had proved that all Hun officers were not of the von Sinzig type.

Several of the rescued Germans could speak English—but they were decidedly reticent. In the back of their minds they rather feared that they were in for a bad time. They knew that their late kapitan had been practically outlawed and that he was "wanted" by the authorities for having, amongst other misdemeanours, destroyed the Fremantle aerodrome by means of an incendiary bomb. They rather expected that they would be blamed for the acts of their fugitive superior.

On the other hand, they were grateful to their rescuers for having saved their lives, and with typical Teutonic reasoning they eventually decided that one way to repay the kindness and to ingratiate themselves in the eyes of the Englishman would be to give away their former officers.

The spokesman led off by informing Sir Reginald Fosterdyke that Unter-Leutnant Hans Leutter was the person who dropped the incendiary bomb from the observation basket in the hope that it would destroy the *Golden Hind*.

"He was, of course, acting under Count von Sinzig's orders," remarked Fosterdyke, drily. "Where is Herr Leutter?"

"Dead," was the reply. "He was one of the three left on Z64."

"And Count von Sinzig was one of the other two?"

The German airman shrugged his shoulders and made a gesture of disgust. He still rankled over his kapitan's cowardly desertion. It was long obvious to all the survivors of Z64 that von Sinzig had no intention of summoning aid. Eight hours had elapsed since he began his flight in the *Albatross*. In that time, he must have sighted several vessels, since the scene of the disaster was not many miles from one of the great Atlantic trade routes.

"Kapitan Count von Sinzig left *Z64* soon after daybreak this morning, mein Herr," replied the German. "At seven o'clock, to be exact."

"Left—how?" demanded Fosterdyke, sharply.

"In an *Albatross* monoplane. He was last seen going east-north-east."

Fosterdyke dismissed his informant and turned to Kenyon and Bramsdean.

"The cunning old rascal!" he exclaimed. "I see his little game now. He's completing the final stage by airplane. I suppose by this time he's won the Chauvasse Prize; but I don't envy him."

"Will you enter a protest, sir?" asked Peter.

"Protest? Not much," replied the baronet, emphatically. "These seventeen Huns can do the protesting if they want to, and I rather fancy they will."

"There's many a slip," quoted Kenyon. "He may not complete the course after all."

CHAPTER XXIII
A DUMPING OPERATION

THE HEAVILY LADEN *Golden Hind* resumed her delayed journey. Both gas-bags and planes had to do their full share of work to keep the airship afloat. She was flying low, but making good progress; but so little was her reserve of buoyancy that had the three Huns who perished in the catastrophe to *Z64* been saved, it was doubtful whether Fosterdyke could have "carried on."

To make matters worse, some of the patches on the repaired ballonets were leaking, for owing to the heat of the rubber the solution was not holding well.

"I wonder if Drake's *Golden Hind*, when she arrived in the Thames after circumnavigating the globe, was patched up like we are," remarked Kenyon. "It took Drake three long years to do the trick, and we look like completing our voyage in under seventeen days."

"If the old 'bus holds out," added Bramsdean. "'Tany rate, no one can say we haven't done our bit. The *Golden Hinds*' been a regular sort of aerial lifeboat. That is some satisfaction. I'd rather we did that than win the race."

"I suppose our passengers won't get up to any of their Hunnish tricks?" observed Kenneth.

"Trust Fosterdyke for that," replied Peter grimly. "He's had 'em placed in the dining-saloon. (Fortunately, we won't require many more meals.) They can amuse themselves there without getting into mischief. There's one of our fellows stationed outside to keep the blighters in order."

Just then the baronet came upon the scene.

"Von Sinzig looks like pulling it off," he observed. "A wireless from the S.S. *Wontwash* reports that a monoplane passed over the ship at 6 P.M., flying east. According to the position given, the *Wontwash* was only thirty-five miles west of Gibraltar."

"Then perhaps he's back at his hangar by this time," commented Peter. "Any news of the others?"

"Yes; Commodore Theodore Nye has been unable to get hold of another 'bus yet, although two of the Australian R.A.F. pilots are bringing him a 'Bristol' machine from Melbourne. He's out of the running. That he admits, but he means to complete the course, even if it takes him six months."

"And the Jap?" asked Kenyon.

"Not a word," replied the baronet. "He's keeping quiet; but mark my words, that quadruplane will turn up unexpectedly. If his 'bus had had British motors, he would have romped home in less than a week."

"What engines has he?" asked Bramsdean.

"Japanese," replied Fosterdyke. "Passable imitations of ours and good up to a certain point; but give me British engines all the jolly old time."

Although the baronet made frequent enquiries of the operator, no wireless messages concerning von Sinzig came through.

"Perhaps he's crashed," suggested Peter.

"Not he," replied Kenyon. "That Hun's got the luck of a cat with nine lives. He's playing his own game."

"It is a game," added Bramsdean. "Loading that crowd of Huns on to us is like a man in a mile race chucking his gear to another competitor and telling him to hang on. I don't wish the blighter any harm, but I do hope that if he pulls off the money prize they'll pay him in German marks at the pre-war rate of exchange. That'd make him look blue!"

Although no news came in concerning their Hun rival, the officers and crew of the *Golden Hind* began to be bombarded with wireless messages from Britons in every quarter of the globe. All were of the most encouraging nature, for the story of Fosterdyke's airship and her adventures and misadventures—all more or less distorted owing to the lack of authentic detail—had awakened world-wide interest.

There were cheery messages from patriotic Britons; incentive ones from sportsmen, to whom the suggestion of a race appealed more than did the fact that the contest was one of endurance calculated to uphold the prestige of British flying men. Frenchmen, Dutchmen, Norwegians, Americans, and Japanese all sent greetings to the intrepid British airmen.

"Didn't know we had so many friends," remarked Fosterdyke. "Sportsmanlike of those Americans and Japs, too, when they have representatives in the show."

The *Golden Hind* was now approaching the regular mail line, where routes to and from the Cape and round the Horn unite in the neighbourhood of Las Palmas.

"We'll signal the first vessel we sight," decided Sir Reginald, "and get her to relieve us of our cargo of Fritzes. The sooner the better, because several of the ballonets are showing distinct symptoms of porosity."

Five minutes later the airship had slowed down and had swung round on a course parallel to a homeward-bound Dutchman.

The skipper of the latter, when appealed to by megaphone, stoutly refused to receive the seventeen Germans. He gave no reason why he should not do so, and without waiting for further parley rang for full speed ahead.

A little later a French auxiliary barque was sighted, bound south. Fosterdyke made no attempt to intercept her.

"There are limits," he observed. "Dumping those Huns on board an outward-bound Frenchman is one of them. Now for the next vessel. Three for luck."

The third was a British tramp, bound from Montevideo for Naples. Her "Old Man," although ignorant that a Round-the-World aerial race was in progress or even in contemplation, readily agreed to help the *Golden Hind* on her way.

"I'll find use for 'em," he added with infinite relish. "They'll work their passage, never you fear. Three times I've been torpedoed without warning, and on two occasions Fritz popped up to jeer at us struggling in waterlogged boats."

While conversation was in progress between Fosterdyke and the master of the S.S. *Diaphanous*, a wire hawser had been lowered from the bows of the airship and made fast to the tramp's after-winch. Since she was steaming dead in the eye of the wind there was no necessity for her to alter helm. The *Golden Hind*, pitching slightly, was towed astern of and thirty feet above the tramp. As the airship's course was almost identical with that of the tramp Fosterdyke conscientiously kept the propellers revolving, since, even in the present circumstances, he did not wish to give his rivals a chance of raising a protest on the score that the flight of the British airship had been mechanically aided.

The seventeen Germans showed no great enthusiasm at being placed on board the tramp. At first they imagined that the *Diaphanous* was bound for the Pacific. Even the prospect of being dumped ashore at Naples was not at all attractive.

When they did make a move they descended the rope-ladder so slowly and deliberately that it was obvious they meant to detain the *Golden Hind* as much as possible.

"I see through their little game," exclaimed Fosterdyke, angrily. "Make 'em get a move on, Jackson."

The Leading Hand wanted no further bidding. Ably seconded by Chief Air Mechanic Hayward, he gave vent to such a flow of forcible language, accompanied by realistic dumbshow, that the Huns changed their tactics completely. It was even necessary to check their impetuosity, lest the ladder should break under the weight of too many men descending simultaneously. Then, with a joyous toot on her syren as the hawser was cast off, and a stentorian greeting from the Mercantile Marine skipper, the *Diaphanous* gathered way, while the *Golden Hind,* almost as buoyant as of yore, rose steadily and rapidly against the gentle breeze.

Two hours later land—the Moroccan coast—was sighted on the starboard bow. Then fifty minutes later Fosterdyke touched Kenyon on the shoulder and pointed dead ahead to a faint object rising above the horizon.

"Guess we've done the trick, barring accidents," he observed. "That's Gibraltar."

CHAPTER XXIV
WITHIN SIGHT OF SUCCESS

COUNT KARL VON SINZIG had not started upon his long solo flight in the *Albatross* without studiously calculating his chances. He knew the machine and its capabilities, and, given ordinary luck, he saw no reason why he should not make a landing on Spanish soil, replenish fuel, and carry on to his hangar in Estremadura before his hated rival arrived at Gibraltar. Even if there were delays in obtaining petrol, he still had a useful lead, thanks to his twelve hours' start in advance of the *Golden Hind.* The two hundred extra miles he had to cover beyond Gibraltar was a mere bagatelle—a question of an hour and twenty minutes' flight.

He rather regretted that the accident to *Z64* had not occurred nearer the African coast; but realising that he was lucky to be able to carry on, he ran the risk of a prolonged flight over the sea with comparative equanimity.

Within an hour of leaving the wrecked Zeppelin he sighted two vessels, but with callous indifference to his promise to his crew he made not the slightest attempt to communicate with either of them. He was "all out" to win the much-needed Chauvasse Prize. Even his indictment by the various Allied Governments hardly worried him. Time to consider what he should do in the matter when he was safe on Spanish soil, he decided.

The *Albatross,* one of the best types of German machines, was practically an automatic flier. Von Sinzig could keep her on her course by an occasional pressure with his feet upon the rudder-bar, thus leaving both hands free. He was able to eat and drink, to study maps and make observations without risk of the monoplane getting out of control, while if needs be he could leave the pilot's seat, knowing that the *Albatross* would hold on automatically for several minutes with only a slight deviation in direction and hardly any difference in altitude.

Although only ten degrees north of the Tropics, it was bitterly cold at ten thousand feet; but the count had taken due precautions to combat the low temperature. He was warmly clad in orthodox flying kit, including sheepskin boots, fleece-lined leather jacket and trousers, all electrically heated. He had four thermos flasks filled with hot coffee and a pocket flask of brandy. For provisions he carried concentrated food, beef lozenges, and Strasburg sausages.

Hour after hour passed. The *Albatross* was flying magnificently, her pilot holding on to a compass course, after making due allowances for the "drift" of the air current. He had based this allowance upon the direction of the wind when he left *Z64*; but unknown to him the light breeze had shifted eight points and was now blowing slightly ahead of his port beam. Then, having backed, it presently veered six points and blew with increasing force right against the *Albatross* ; but von Sinzig was for the present in ignorance of the fact. Had he known that instead of a following breeze of about twenty miles an hour there was a head wind approaching the neighbourhood of thirty-five miles, he would not have been so chock-a-block with confidence.

When, at the end of the time limit he had set, he was not in sight of land he began to feel anxious. Half an hour later, as he was still without a glimpse of the coast, his misgivings increased, but ten minutes later he picked up land on his right. This was a puzzle. He had expected to make a landfall right ahead, and its appearance in an unexpected quarter mystified him. In point of fact he was in the neighbourhood of Cape Blanco, or nearly 250 miles south of Cape St. Vincent, where he hoped to pass over on his way to Estremadura.

A knowledge of the Moroccan coast obtained during a cruise in a German gunboat at the time of the Agadir crisis stood von Sinzig in good stead. He was able to recognise certain landmarks in spite of viewing them from a different aspect, and accordingly he turned the monoplane in a north-easterly direction, keeping parallel to the African coast, The new direction would take him a little to the eastward of Cadiz; rather nearer that port than Gibraltar. He had not the slightest inclination to fly over the latter fortress. Rather vaguely he wondered whether he would sight the *Golden Hind* making thither, since, sooner or later, unless a mishap occurred, the rival aviators must cut each other's routes.

He was now painfully aware of the change of wind. The direction of the smoke from several steamers, and the sight of a full-rigged ship running in a south-westerly direction told him that. Additionally, as he saw by the aid of his binoculars, that sailing ship was running under topsails only. That meant something more than a stiff breeze—and against this he had to contend.

Suddenly he detected an ominous cough of the motor. He knew that the petrol supply was running low, but he had no idea that the gauge registered so little. The tank was practically empty.

"Himmel!" gasped the dumfounded Hun. "Will she last out?"

He mentally measured the distance between him and the Spanish coast. A good ten miles. With a following wind he could glide that distance from that altitude, but not with this infernal head wind!

The engine was running jerkily. Clearly its spasmodic coughing betokened the fact that it would soon cease duty from sheer inanition. Its life-blood was being cut off at the heart of the machine—its petrol tank. That head wind. How von Sinzig cursed it! Had it been in his favour, even if he failed to volplane as far as the shore, the *Albatross,* being provided with floats, could have drifted on the surface.

In the midst of his incoherent utterances von Sinzig realised that the motor had at last given out. He trimmed the ailerons and prepared for a long glide, but, as he had feared, the head wind made it a matter of impossibility for the *Albatross* to cover more than two miles before she alighted.

It did not take long to complete the volplane, although the pilot nursed his machine to the best of his ability in the hope of prolonging the oblique descent.

The *Albatross* "landed" badly, her floats striking the water with a resounding smack. The count, having done his best, could do no more. He sat smoking a cigarette and keeping a look out for a vessel that would come to his assistance. There were several away to the south'ard, for he had alighted well to the north'ard of the regular steamer track between Gibraltar and Cape St. Vincent. They were too far off to notice the little *Albatross.*

Then von Sinzig made the disconcerting discovery that the starboard float was leaking. Already, owing to this cause, the monoplane was listing so that her starboard wingtip was touching the water. This fact, combined with the knowledge that he was momentarily drifting farther and farther away from land, did not tend to improve the Hun's peace of mind.

Half an hour later, during which time the monoplane had drifted at least three miles, and was being considerably buffeted by the rising sea, von Sinzig noticed that a vessel was bearing down upon the crippled *Albatross.*

As she approached, the count saw that she was a small motor-yacht of about forty or fifty tons, and that she was flying the burgee of the "Real Club Mediterraneo" and the Spanish ensign. The sight of the Spanish colours gave von Sinzig renewed hope.

The yacht slowed down and lost way a few yards to the wind'ard of the monoplane. For so small a vessel she carried a large crew. There were half a dozen men for'ard, clad in white canvas jumpers and trousers and wearing red woollen caps. Aft were two gorgeously attired individuals in gold-laced yachting uniforms.

Von Sinzig, who was a fair Spanish linguist, hailed them. A rope thrown from the bows of the yacht fell across the nose of the *Albatross*. This the count caught and secured.

"Can you supply me with petrol, señor?" asked von Sinzig. "My tank is empty. A hundred litres will be enough."

One of the gold-laced men shook his head and extended his hands, palms uppermost.

"I am desolated at being compelled to refuse your excellency's modest request," he replied, "but we have paraffin engines and carry only a small quantity of petrol for starting purposes. How far have you come?"

"Nearly round the world," replied the Hun, grandiloquently. He could not resist the typically Teutonic trait of self-advertisement.

"Dios!" exclaimed the Spaniard, twirling his long moustachios. "Then you are Count Karl von Sinzig, who left Quintanur, in the province of Estremadura, sixteen or seventeen days ago?"

"I am," admitted von Sinzig, proudly.

The Spaniard said a few words in an undertone to his companion. The other's eyes gleamed and he nodded his head vigorously.

"We will take you on board and tow your machine," announced the owner of the yacht.

"To Cadiz or Huelva?" asked the count.

"Accept ten thousand regrets, count," replied the Spaniard. "We must take you to Gibraltar."

"But I have no wish to be taken to Gibraltar," declared von Sinzig. "I will give a thousand pesetas to be landed at Cadiz."

The Don again shrugged his shoulders.

"No doubt my crew would be glad of your offer of a thousand pesetas, count," he replied, "but since they know that the English have offered a reward equal to five thousand pesetas—"

"You would sell me?" demanded von Sinzig, furiously.

"I sell you, señor? Not I—a caballero of Spain! You insult me by the suggestion. I recollect, however, that I once had a brother. He was lost at sea, while travelling on an English vessel from New York to Cadiz. Like you, he wanted to land at Cadiz, but he was not able to do so. For why? Because the ship was torpedoed by one of your ever-accursed U-boats. Therefore I have a small measure of revenge when I hand you over to the English authorities at Gibraltar. Be pleased, señor, to step aboard."

Covered by an automatic pistol, Count Karl von Sinzig had no option but to obey. In the race round the world he was down and out.

CHAPTER XXV
FIRE!

SIR REGINALD FOSTERDYKE LAID down his pencil and uttered an exclamation of intense satisfaction. He had just "shot the sun" and had finished working out his position.

"Another hour will see us at Gib., lads," he announced joyously. "Then there'll be some mafficking. What's your programme? Going to pack your suit cases and back by the Madrid-Paris express?"

"You are not leaving the *Golden Hind* at Gibraltar?" asked Kenneth.

"No," replied the baronet. "But I must certainly get some repairs executed before I resume my flight to England. I thought, perhaps, you were in a hurry to get home."

"There's no immediate hurry, sir," declared the chums, simultaneously.

"A few more days won't matter," began Kenyon; but before he could proceed with his explanation the alarm bell rang violently and continuously.

"What's wrong now?" exclaimed Fosterdyke, snatching up the voice tube.

Peter, glancing aft through the window of the navigation room, which being raised gave a clear view over the roof of the rest of the nacelle, saw at once what was amiss.

Dense volumes of smoke, tinged with dull red flames, were pouring from the after-end of the fuselage. Fanned by the rush of the airship, the black vapour was streaming in its wake like a fox's tail.

Leaving Kenyon to take charge of the navigation room and cautioning him to keep the *Golden Hind* dead in the eye of the wind, and as fast as she could possibly go, Fosterdyke and Peter hastened aft.

They found the alleyway thick with smoke, for on the well-known principle that "the wind follows the ship" the draught was carrying the fumes within the nacelle in a forward direction.

A man wearing a smoke helmet brushed past them. It was Hayward going to find some fire-extinguishers. Others of the crew, who had hastily donned masks to protect themselves from the choking vapour, were busily engaged in hurling pyrene into the seat of the conflagration.

Although the speed of the *Golden Hind* through the air fanned the flames, Fosterdyke had done well to order speed to be maintained. The velocity had the effect of compelling the fire to trail astern instead of spreading upwards and thus destroying the envelope. Even as it was the heat had caused the non-inflammable brodium to expand, giving the envelope a tendency to trim down by the head.

"Petrol tank to No. 5 motor, sir," reported a grimy and perspiring mechanic, who through sheer exhaustion and being partly gassed by the noxious fumes had to withdraw from the fray. "Went up all of a sudden, like. Never saw such a flare up in all my life, sir; but we're getting it under."

It was indeed a stiff fight. In a few seconds the area of the fire had attained such large dimensions that it was impossible to reach the actual source. The fire-fighters had first to subdue the fringe of the conflagration, and by the time they had done this several of them were *hors de combat* by reason of the suffocating gases thrown off by the oxygen-exterminating pyrene. Above the crackling of the flames came the sharp tang of the suspension wires holding the nacelle to the aluminium envelope as they parted under the terrific heat.

Not only were the crew faced with the danger of the fire getting the upper hand; the while there was the chance of a portion of the fuselage becoming detached from the gas-bag, and the prospect of being hurled through space from a height of eight or nine thousand feet above the sea was one that might well in cold blood put fear into the heart of the bravest of the brave. But in the heat of action the crew, knowing the danger, faced the risk manfully. Working in relays, they plied the flames with the fire-extinguishing chemicals. As fast as one man fell out, temporarily overcome by the fumes and the terrific heat, another took his place until the fire was overcome. Even then the danger was not over. There was still a possibility of the smouldering fuselage being fanned into a blaze. Parts of the aluminium framework and panelling were warped and twisted into fantastic shapes. Snake-like coils of wire indicated the fact that several of the highly important connections between the fuselage and the envelope had been burnt through. Whether a sufficient number of tension wires remained to adequately support the afterpart of the nacelle remained a matter of doubt.

Unaccountably the petrol tank feeding No. 5 motor had taken fire. The pipes and unions had been frequently examined and found to be in good order. In fact, Hayward had personally inspected the fittings of that particular tank less than a quarter of an hour before the outbreak.

The damage was serious. Both Nos. 5 and 6 motors were out of action, the former showing signs of crashing through the charred framework of the fuselage. The flames had spread to Fosterdyke's cabin, completely gutting it.

Only a few aluminium frames were left, and these, blackened and bent, trailed forlornly astern like a gaunt skeleton.

With the contraction of the brodium after the fire had been quelled the envelope, instead of tending to tilt aft, now showed a tendency to droop. The heat had melted the solder of the union pipes through which the gas was passed either to or from the metal pressure flasks, and several thousand feet of brodium had escaped.

Driven only by four propellers, her preciously scanty supply of brodium sadly depleted, and with the controls of the two after planes damaged by the flames, the *Golden Hind* was in a perilous state. She was just able, and no more, to overcome the attraction of gravity. How long she would be able to maintain herself in the air was a problem of supposition.

Had the *Golden Hind* been supported by hydrogen gas nothing could have saved her. The overcoming of the flames was a triumph for the fire-resisting properties of brodium. The patent gas had been put to one of the severest tests—an actual fire in mid-air—and had emerged with flying colours.

From the time of the alarm being raised until the fire was subdued only half an hour had elapsed. The smoke-grimed and fatigued crew were glad to rest, while Fosterdyke and Peter returned to the navigation room, there to wash and replace their singed and reeking clothes with others from Kenyon's and Bramsdean's kit-bags. The baronet had to borrow a suit. The one he was wearing was in holes, while all his others on board were destroyed when his cabin was burnt out.

Fosterdyke was cheerful. In fact he was jocular. He realised that things might have been far worse; he was glad to find that the *Golden Hind* was still navigable and that none of his crew had sustained injury.

"This comes of boasting, Kenyon," he remarked. "I said we'd be in Gib. in an hour. We stood a chance of being in 'Kingdom Come.' What's she doing now?"

"Not more than eighty, sir," replied Kenneth, "and we've a stiffish wind to contend with."

"Eighty, eh? Not so dusty, considering we're trailing the wreckage of my cabin astern, and there's only four props to shove us along. She's dipping, though."

"She is, sir," agreed Kenyon, gravely. "I've trimmed the planes to their maximum. That tends to shove her nose up, but if I didn't she'd sit on her tail."

"We'll finish at the tape like an aerial Cleopatra's Needle," declared Fosterdyke. "Hello! There's Tangier. That strip of blue you can just see beyond is the Straits of Gibraltar. We're a bit to the east'ard of our course."

Another half an hour of strenuous battling against heavy odds brought the *Golden Hind* immediately to the west of Ceuta. Ahead could be discerned the famous rock, although viewed from an altitude and "end on" its well-known appearance as a lion couchant was absent. But the *Golden Hind* had shot her bolt. "We're baulked at the tape," declared Fosterdyke. "This head wind's doing us. Hard lines, but we must take things as we find them."

Like von Sinzig he had been beaten by the head wind, but Fosterdyke, instead of raving and cursing like his German rival, accepted the situation philosophically. It was hard lines, failing within sight of the goal; but the baronet kept a stiff upper lip. He had done everything humanly possible to achieve his aim. He could do no more.

The *Golden Hind*, inclined at an angle of sixty degrees, was dropping slowly but surely. With her remaining motors running all out she was unable to overcome the pull of gravity. Even as she dropped, her progress towards her goal was maintained at a rate of a bare five miles an hour above and against that of the wind.

Every man on board was holding on like grim death. With the floor as steep as the roof of a house there was nothing to be done but hold on. The ballonets were practically empty save the four or five for'ard ones. The propellers were now virtually helices—whirling screws that strove valiantly but unavailingly to lift the huge bulk of the airship in an almost vertical direction. Should the motors fail to function, then the *Golden Hind* would drop like a stone. As it was she was falling surely and slowly.

Already officers and men had donned their inflated India-rubber lifebelts. There was not the slightest sign of panic. The men, although keenly disappointed at failure within sight of success, were joking with each other.

"Stand by to jump, all hands," shouted Fosterdyke. "Keep clear of the raffle, and you'll be as right as rain. There are half a dozen vessels within a couple of miles of us."

Some of the men slid along the sloping alleyway to the side doors. Others tore away the large celluloid windows in the cabins and motor-rooms, so as to be able to jump clear directly the fuselage touched the water.

The two chums had drawn themselves through the windows of the navigation room and were standing on the blunt bows and steadying themselves by the tension wires running from the normal top of the nacelle to the underside of the envelope.

With the four motors running to the last the *Golden Hind* dropped into the sea. Her projecting envelope was the first to come into contact with the water. The ballonets, practically air-tight compartments, checked the downward movement, while the whole of the hitherto inclined bulk, pivoted as it were by the water-borne stern, dropped until it resumed its normal horizontal position.

Fosterdyke alone had remained in the navigation room. Directly he saw that the airship was resting temporarily on the surface and was beginning to gather way like a gigantic hydroplane he switched off the remaining motors.

"Every man for himself," he shouted.

CHAPTER XXVI
"WELL PLAYED, SIR!"

WATER POURED INTO THE open doors and windows and through the charred and torn stern of the nacelle.

The aluminium envelope, not built to withstand abnormal stress, began buckling amidships. Tension wires, no longer in tension but in compression, were spreading in all directions as the huge gas-bag settled down upon the already foundering nacelle.

Every one of the crew realised the danger of being entangled in the wreckage. In a trice the water was dotted with heads and shoulders of life-belted swimmers as the crew struck out to get clear of the sinking airship, and presently Fosterdyke was surrounded by a little mob of undaunted men.

"Thank heaven!" said the baronet, after a hasty count. "None missing. Keep together, lads, there's a vessel bearing down on us."

Not one but four craft were hastening to the rescue. Amongst these was the T.B.D. *Zeebrugge*, which, eighteen days previously, had gone to search for the derelict *Golden Hind* and had placed Sir Reginald Fosterdyke on board.

Fortunately, the water was warm, and in spite of a fairly high sea running the late crew of the *Golden Hind* were taken aboard the destroyer.

Fosterdyke and the others, declining to go below, stood on deck and watched the end of the airship that had taken them safely for nearly twenty-eight thousand miles, to perish within five miles of the Rock of Gibraltar, her official starting-point.

The end was not long delayed. The buckling of the aluminium envelope resulted in ballonet after ballonet collapsing under the pressure of water. The fuselage had already disappeared. Bow and stern, nearly four hundred feet apart, reared themselves high in the air; then, with a terrific rush of mingled brodium and air that caused a seething cauldron around each of the extremities of the envelope, the last of the *Golden Hind* sank beneath the waves.

"Rough luck losing such a fine airship," commiserated the Lieut.-Commander of the destroyer.

"It is," agreed Fosterdyke, feelingly. "Especially as she is my own design and I superintended every bit of her construction. It was a pity, too, we didn't hang on for another half an hour. I'd have jockeyed her over the Rock somehow."

"It was a brilliant achievement, Sir Reginald," said the naval officer. "Every sportsman will sympathise with you, but I'm sure they'll shout: 'Well played, sir!'"

"Any news of the other competitors?" asked Peter.

"Yes. Commodore Nye, the Yankee, is still stranded in Australia, but I suppose you know that. Count Hyashi, the Jap, crashed somewhere near Saigon. He, too, was almost home."

"Jolly hard lines," murmured Kenyon, sympathetically. "Was he hurt?"

"No, hardly bruised, but a bit shaken. Engine failure, they say," continued the Lieut.-Commander. "That leaves only the Hun to be accounted for."

"And I suppose he's completed the circuit?" remarked Fosterdyke, questioningly.

The naval officer laughed.

"Completing the circuit of a prison-yard!" he exclaimed. "That's about his mark. A Spanish yacht brought Count von Sinzig in this morning and handed him over to the Port Admiral. It'll be a three years' job, I fancy. Huns must learn that they can't bomb British air stations in peace time with impunity."

The destroyer ran alongside the dockyard. Fosterdyke and the rest of his crew disembarked. On the jetty they were met by several of the chief Naval, Military, and Air Force officials and two representatives of the International Air Board.

Fosterdyke looked puzzled. He didn't want commiseration, but congratulation seemed a bit out of place.

"On what grounds, Admiral?" he asked.

"On winning the Chauvasse Prize for completing the circumnavigation of the globe," replied the senior International Air Board representative, speaking instead of the Port Admiral. "Fact! You've won it fairly and squarely."

"But—" began the astonished baronet.

"You have," persisted the official. "Do you recollect when the airship broke adrift? The destroyer went in pursuit and put you on board. That was within three miles or so of Ceuta. The same destroyer picks you up out of the water five miles from 'Gib.' Consequently, you've more than completed the circuit, and although the official start was from Gibraltar I don't think there will be any difficulty in obtaining the International Air Board's decision to the effect that you've won."

And that was exactly what happened. Had it not been for Count von Sinzig's underhand work in employing Enrico Jaures to cast adrift the *Gold-*

en Hind, Fosterdyke would not have completed his aerial voyage round the world. By the irony of fate, the Hun had enabled his rival to score.

Fosterdyke won the Chauvasse Prize and the honour of being the first man to fly round the world. Needless to say Kenyon and Bramsdean and the rest of the crew were not forgotten. Honours were heaped upon the intrepid airmen. They were lionised, fêted, and praised to such an extent that they were in danger of developing "swelled heads."

But Kenyon and Bramsdean knew that the achievement would be but a nine days' wonder. Having attempted and won, they were content to return to their profession, their financial standing much increased by their shares in the big prize. They had enough honours and diplomas to satisfy them, but what they prized most was a certificate from the Royal Humane Society for saving the crew of the *Hilda P. Murchison.*

"So, after all," declared Kenyon, "we did do something useful, old son!"